THE LOVE THAT HEALS

Dr Kate Ross thinks she's doing the right thing when she moves from the city to a quiet seaside practice with her father. She hopes the change of scenery will bring about a miracle following the devastating accident four years previously when he'd lost his wife and his will to live. When her senior partner, Dr Cory Lawrence, offers to help, she jumps at the chance. But is it for the right reasons, or will it just end in more heartache for them all?

Books by Teresa Ashby
in the Linford Romance Library:

TERESA ASHBY

THE LOVE
THAT HEALS

Complete and Unabridged

LINFORD
Leicester

First published in Great Britain in 2009

First Linford Edition
published 2015

A catalogue record for this book is available
from the British Library.

ISBN 978–1–4448–2368–4

Published by
F. A. Thorpe (Publishing)
Anstey, Leicestershire

Set by Words & Graphics Ltd.
Anstey, Leicestershire
Printed and bound in Great Britain by
T. J. International Ltd., Padstow, Cornwall

This book is printed on acid-free paper

1

Dr Kate Ross was just checking her messages at the reception desk on her way out of the health centre, when a warm voice spoke in her ear. 'I have tickets for the new show by The Wyatt's Cove Theatre Group this evening. What do you say, Kate? Will you come with me?'

Kate turned slowly to face Dr Cory Lawrence, an excuse already springing to her lips as had become her habit whenever anyone asked her for a date. Only this time it was so much harder to say no, because she really liked him.

'I'm sorry, I can't make it tonight,' she said politely. *Any other time, any other life*, she thought, *and I'd leap at the chance of a date with you.*

'Oh, go on, Kate,' he said. 'Why don't you come along? It'll be fun.'

'I really can't,' she said. 'I'm tied up every evening.'

'No matter. Perhaps some other time,' he said with a smile and strode away down the corridor to his room.

Kate let out her breath in a long sigh. If she'd thought coming to Wyatt's Cove was going to be the easy option, she'd been very much mistaken.

Hurrying over to the reception desk, she leaned across and spoke to the receptionist. 'I'm off now, Gaynor. I'll do my home visits, then the hospital rounds. I should be back well before afternoon surgery.'

'Right you are, Kate,' Gaynor said with her usual chirpy smile, and Kate couldn't help thinking how nice everyone here was; how friendly and kind they'd been to her since her arrival.

'Kate.'

She stopped in her tracks and turned back to the receptionist. 'Was there something else?' she asked, glancing at her watch.

'I couldn't help overhearing,' Gaynor

said. 'Why don't you go with him? It couldn't hurt, could it?'

Kate laughed incredulously. 'I'm sorry?'

'I know it's not for me to say, but . . . '

'As I told Dr Lawrence, I can't make it tonight,' Kate said.

Gaynor clicked her tongue and was about to say something else when the telephone rang.

Hurrying out to her car, Kate wondered if coming to Wyatt's Cove had been a mistake. She'd never even heard of the place until a colleague practically thrust the advertisement under her nose.

'It'll be ideal for you and your father,' Tom Harrison had said. 'Nice quiet little town on the coast, close-knit community. Just think — no more night calls to seedy estates; no more getting mugged for the contents of your medical bag.'

'Anyone would think you wanted to get rid of me,' Kate had laughed. But even so, her interest was well and truly kindled. It sounded perfect, just as Tom said. And he was right — she was frightened whenever it was her turn to be duty doctor. And there were always those occasions when you had to decide whether that 'emergency' call was genuine, or a hoax.

'Not at all,' Tom replied. 'You're a good GP and I'd be sorry to lose you, but I'm thinking of what's best for you, not what's best for this practice.'

As Tom said, a nice, quiet little seaside community would be ideal, and her father had always loved the sea.

Wyatt's Cove was on a peninsula with rocky cliffs at one end and sprawling marshes and quiet sandy beaches on either side. The first time she'd driven to the town, she'd had an impression of foaming white water as the North Sea smashed against the rocks. If the unexpected beauty of the place hadn't convinced her to make the move, then the set-up at the health centre would. The main building was an old manor house which, despite being turned into a hospital, had retained much of its old character and charm. It nestled in the afternoon sunshine, dark beams against cream rendering beneath a warm red roof.

It was small but more or less self-sufficient, with its own x-ray department and a number of small wards. There was also an operating theatre for emergencies and simple routine surgery. Anyone requiring major surgery or specialist treatment had to travel to the General Hospital some thirty miles away.

Annexed to the old house was a modern single-storey extension. This was the clinic where Kate had joined the practice headed by Dr Cory Lawrence.

She climbed into her car, recalling the first time she'd met Dr Lawrence. In his mid-thirties, he was much younger than she'd been expecting and he'd greeted her with the most welcoming of smiles. He had the most attractive dark grey eyes, which were filled with warmth. She hadn't been able to help warming to him. For the past month, since she'd taken up her post here, he'd been wonderful helping her to settle in. And then today, he'd asked her out. A perfectly innocent invitation, but it set alarm bells ringing in her mind. She simply couldn't afford to get involved with anyone. The smile faded and she directed her mind on the morning ahead.

After making her first home visit, Kate hurried out into the bright May sunshine and took in a deep breath of fresh air. She could smell the sea and taste the tang of salt on her lips. How different life was here to her former post in an inner-city practice. She paused and looked out over the sea, which today was deep green, its surface scattered with white foam where gulls wheeled and dived, their wings glinting silver in the sunlight.

Few places on the peninsula weren't in sight of the sea. And from her own bungalow she had the most beautiful view, one she felt she would never tire of seeing. A sudden gust of wind caught her hair and she hurried back to her car. 'Dragged through a hedge backwards' was a phrase that leapt to mind as she examined her reflection in the rear-view mirror. Quickly, she combed through her short, dark, shiny locks until she looked presentable again. There was a healthy dab of pink in her cheeks and a shine in her dark brown eyes that had been absent for far too long. Nothing whatsoever to do with Cory Lawrence, she told herself firmly. It was this place, this town.

She was on her way to the next patient when the call came through from the clinic on her mobile phone. 'Are you anywhere near Rosemary Villas?' Gaynor asked urgently. 'We've just had a call from Mrs Brown. She thinks her husband's having a heart attack. Can you make it there quickly?'

'I'm on my way,' Kate said. 'What number?'

'No number. It's a terrace of four and you want one of the middle ones. It's called Rose Cottage.'

Kate had spent some time familiarising herself with the narrow twisting roads in the town and arrived at Rosemary Villas within six minutes. Just as she was getting out of her car Cory pulled up in his, and together they raced towards the front door, which was opened before either could knock.

Kate hesitated for a fraction of a second and Cory put out his hand. 'Your patient,' he said with a deferential smile.

Clearly Mr Brown was in considerable pain, sitting on the floor leaning back against an armchair. His wife, a sprightly woman in her sixties, said, 'I knew it wasn't an angina attack, because he was just sitting there when it happened. He gets the angina when he's been overdoing it. I gave him one of his angina pills, though, and when it didn't work, I gave him another.'

'I'm going to give you an injection to

ease the pain,' Kate said, opening her bag. 'You'll feel better almost immediately, Mr Brown.' She was aware of Cory watching her every move and had to make a conscious effort to steady her hand. 'I'm going to send for an ambulance and have you admitted to the General Hospital,' she said. 'You'll have to spend at least the next few days in the coronary care unit. After that, if you're doing well, we'll have you moved back to the hospital here to convalesce.'

Kate picked up her mobile phone, but Cory put out his hand. 'It's done, Kate,' he said.

'Thank you, Dr Lawrence,' she said with a forced smile. 'But I wish you hadn't done that.'

Within ten minutes Mr Brown was in a lot less pain, and by the time the ambulance arrived the patient was already looking a little better. Relieved of the pain and pressure, some of the fear had gone from his eyes.

Mrs Brown went with him in the ambulance and as Kate and Cory were leaving Rose Cottage, the next-door neighbour called to them over the fence. 'Poor old Jack, was it? Heart I suppose?'

'He'll be all right now, Mrs Ferguson, don't you worry,' Cory said cheerfully. 'Is everything all right with you?'

'Oh, I muddle along, you know. That's the new doctor, is it?' She looked Kate up and down.

'Indeed it is,' Cory said, grinning. 'Mrs Ferguson, this is Dr Ross. Dr Ross, this is Maisie Ferguson.'

'Pleased to meet you I'm sure,' Mrs Ferguson said, frowning. 'Bit young, isn't she? Are you sure she's a proper doctor?'

'Absolutely,' Cory said, his grin widening. 'You know how we are at the practice. We only take on the best.'

Mrs Ferguson chuckled. 'Have you time for a cup of tea, Doctors?'

'I think so,' Cory said, taking Kate's arm. 'You're not in a hurry, are you, Kate?'

'Well, I . . . '

'Good, that's settled then. Put the kettle on, Mrs F, we'll be right round.'

'What did you do that for?' Kate said as he steered her out of one gate and in through the next. 'I've calls to make, I can't just . . . '

'Of course you can. It's what working somewhere like this is all about.'

'But I . . . '

'There.' Mrs Ferguson smiled happily as she handed them a cup each. She chatted nineteen to the dozen while Cory listened attentively, his grey eyes apparently deeply interested. Kate looked discreetly at her watch.

'I really should be off,' she said. 'I still have a few house calls to make.'

'And so should I,' Cory said, standing up. 'Thanks for the tea, Mrs F.'

Once they were outside standing beside their cars, he said, 'She's lonely. She doesn't go out much and it doesn't hurt to let her chat for a while.'

'We're doctors, not social workers,' Kate said. 'It's not our place.'

'You've worked in the inner city too

long, Kate,' he said. 'You've forgotten that patients are people.'

'She's not even my patient and I've just wasted half an hour . . . '

'Not wasted, Kate, no,' he said, shaking his head. 'Time spent on people is never time wasted.'

The bright sun beat down on them, turning his hair to a halo of spun gold. He reached into his breast pocket and took out a pair of sunglasses. Kate felt oddly disconcerted once his eyes were hidden. His lips were curved upwards at the corners with little half moon lines running outwards across his craggy face — too smooth to be called lived-in, but too rough to be called classic.

'I have a lot to get through today,' she muttered.

'What's happened to you, Kate? When you came down here for the interview, I thought . . . '

He broke off and she wished she could see his eyes. Was he angry, upset — what? Did he regret taking her on? Was that it?

'What did you think Cory?'

'I thought you'd fit in here, but you don't seem to want to be a part of this community. I've done my best to draw you in, but you rebuke me at every turn. What else am I to do, Kate?'

'You don't have to integrate me into the community,' she said, her tone softening. 'I'm not your responsibility. It's just that I have a life outside work and I really don't have any time to spare.'

'All right, granted, you don't want any interference in your private life. But when I told you an ambulance was on the way, you were angry. Why, Kate?' Kate felt tears stab at her eyes and she turned away, but he caught hold of her arm and pulled her back round to face him. 'Well?'

'I once asked an ambulance to meet me when I was attending an emergency,' she said so softly he had to stoop low to catch her words. 'The call was a hoax, the paramedics were mugged and the ambulance was stolen.

It was a mistake I never made again.'

He softened his grip on her arm. 'I'm sorry,' he murmured. 'I didn't know.'

'There's a lot you don't know about me,' she said. 'In my last practice, I had to make a lot of very difficult decisions. A late-night call-out to a child with a soaring temperature to a building with the lifts out of action could be a nightmare.'

'I'm sorry, Kate. I didn't realise.'

'No, I'm the one that should be sorry, Cory,' she said at last. 'It's so different here. I'll get used to it.'

'It's still early days,' he said. 'Give yourself a bit more time. But I meant what I said about you becoming part of the community. I found it difficult myself at first. I came here after spending a bit of time with the Red Cross. It was a harrowing experience, especially the time I spent . . . ' He broke off and for a moment his mouth twisted in pain. Kate's heart began to thud as she waited for him to continue. When he did, his voice was steady again. 'Coming here to this quiet little haven was quite a shock to the system at first. And when I was told I'd have to host a garden party for the Hospital Friends, I was dead set against it. Now it's an annual event and I look forward to it. This place has the ability to change you, Kate. It changed me.'

Kate wished she knew him well enough to ask about his experiences overseas. 'I really should be on my way,' she said at last. 'But I will try harder to fit in.'

2

The rest of the morning passed quickly. All her patients were easily dealt with and at last, she returned to do her hospital rounds. She had only two patients to see: a young woman who had had her first baby the day before, and a man convalescing after treatment for a brain tumour. Happy with their progress, she returned to reception to check out again before going home for lunch, but as she was leaving the building she bumped into Cory on his way in.

'Hi.' He grinned. 'Are you going to lunch now?'

'Yes,' she replied guardedly.

'Me too,' he said. 'I don't suppose you'd care to join me? I was going to pop in to the Anchor. They do an excellent ploughman's.'

'I'm afraid I can't.'

'Strictly business,' he interrupted. 'No ulterior motives, I promise you.'

'I really am sorry, Cory,' she said firmly. 'I promised my father I'd be home for lunch on time today. I can't let him down.'

'I understand. But I do need to talk to you, Kate. Could you spare me five minutes after afternoon surgery?'

'Of course,' she replied.

It was a short drive from the medical centre to her bungalow. It stood halfway up a steep incline, huge double-glazed picture windows looking out over the sea. From the window they could see the area where a small colony of seals basked in the sunshine.

She'd fallen in love with it on sight and knew it would be ideal for her father. Now it was getting warmer, she hoped he'd be able to sit out on the veranda, soaking up the sunshine. Perhaps here it would be possible to rekindle his interest in life.

Hurrying in, she went straight to the living room and called out a greeting, but he didn't hear her. Pausing in the doorway, she gazed sadly at him. He was sitting in his wheelchair staring out to sea. There was something so horribly lonely and sad about the back of his head, the thinning grey hair combed neatly back behind his ears. He was so vulnerable now, and she longed to rush in and give him the biggest hug he'd had in his life. Well, why not.

She dashed in, but instead of welcoming her embrace, he began to struggle free of it. Feeling foolish, she backed away from him, hurting like a child rejected by an impatient parent.

'You made me jump.' he said accusingly. 'I didn't hear you come in.' Then suddenly, as if he saw the hurt he'd caused, his face softened into a smile. 'I'm glad you're home, love.'

He wasn't the easiest of patients — doctors seldom were, Kate thought. The car accident which had taken her mother's life almost four years ago had also changed her father's beyond recognition. It had left him with no feeling in his legs and limited use of his arms. Head injuries had left him with several problems, the worst of which was an inability to concentrate.

'What do you fancy for lunch, Pa?' she asked. 'Would you like onion soup and crusty French bread? Or would you prefer salad and quiche?'

He shrugged his shoulders and returned his gaze to the sea. 'I'm so bored, Kate,' he said, his voice tight. 'So sick and tired of sitting in this chair. I can't even take a bath without help.'

Kate's heart sank. He'd been quite cheerful since they'd moved to Wyatt's Cove, but now he seemed to be slipping back again. It was hardly surprising. He had been an active, intelligent man before the accident, but now he couldn't even read a page of a book before his concentration started to slip.

'I thought I heard voices,' he said.

'Hello, Mrs Mayes,' Kate said, turning to face their housekeeper. She didn't know how she'd have managed without her help. Beatrice Mayes was a slim, attractive widow who lived locally. Kate had chosen her very carefully, knowing her father wouldn't stand for a woman who was in the least motherly. He couldn't stand being pampered or made a fuss of, and Mrs Mayes hid her warm heart beneath a brisk and business-like exterior.

'I thought we could have onion soup and French bread for lunch. I picked this loaf up from the baker's on the way here.'

'Don't you worry about lunch; I'll see to that,' Mrs Mayes said cheerfully as she took the bread. She cast a meaningful look at David Ross. 'You stay in here and talk to your father,' she added, keeping her voice low. 'He's been really down in the dumps this morning. I tried to get him to watch the television, but he said if he sees another celebrity going on about what a hard life they've had, he'll . . . '

'Go right round the bend,' he finished for her with a low chuckle.

Kate sat down beside him. Whenever

she sat here, looking out over the sea, she always thought she'd be happy to do it all day, but knew in reality it would drive her slowly mad.

'Why don't you come down to the day centre at the hospital, Pa?' she said.

'And make baskets?' he said scornfully. 'No thanks, Kate. I'm not that far gone yet.'

'It's not like that and you know it,' she scolded him gently. 'You'd get to meet new people, perhaps make some friends.'

'No,' he stated firmly. 'I don't want to go anywhere.'

'Oh, Pa,' she sighed. 'You're not being fair on yourself. You've got to . . . '

'Pull myself together?' he finished for her.

'You know that's the last thing I'd tell you to do,' she said.

'Oh, I'm sorry, Kate,' he said. He looked anguished. His frown deepened and he shook his head slowly. 'People like me always take out our frustrations on those we love the most. And I do love you, Kate, more than anything in the world.'

'I know that, Pa,' she said, her throat aching. 'I love you, too. That's why . . . '

'Lunch is ready,' Mrs Mayes called out.

That's why I brought you here, Kate was about to say. But it hadn't worked, except on a temporary basis. She might just as well have taken him on holiday somewhere.

Getting to her feet, she turned her father's wheelchair around and pushed it towards the dining area at the far end of the room. It was a huge room, divided by a bricked archway which also formed part of a large fireplace. The other rooms were quite small, as if whoever had built the bungalow had done so solely for the view.

Mrs Mayes set a basketful of bread in the centre of the table, then returned with two steaming bowls of soup.

'Aren't you going to join us, Mrs Mayes?' Kate asked.

'I'll have mine in the kitchen later, when the doctor is having his afternoon nap,' she said. 'Do you need any help with that, Doctor?' she added as she tucked a large linen napkin into the neck of his pullover.

'No, I don't,' he growled.

'Please yourself.' She didn't take offence if David was less than polite, but she didn't stand any nonsense from him either. Kate liked her and could congratulate herself that at least where the choice of a housekeeper was concerned, she'd done the right thing.

'Would you butter me a piece of bread, Kate, please?' he asked.

'Of course,' she said, pleased.

If only he would ask for her help more often, or accept it when it was offered, instead of being so stubborn. She'd tried putting herself in his shoes, imagining what it must be like to be suddenly almost wholly dependant on one's child for everything, but it was hard to envisage. He'd always been such an active man, always rushing here and there. He loved everything he did, whether it was his work as a GP, pottering in the garden or playing a round of golf. Whatever he did, he'd always enjoyed it to the full until the accident. He'd lost the only woman he'd ever loved, and the joy in him had been wiped away.

'Did you have a busy morning?' he asked as they ate.

'Rather quiet, really,' she said. 'One of my patients had a heart attack, but he's making good progress at the General. Apart from that, nothing major.'

'No junkies and drop-outs then,' he said with a wry grin.

'No, Pa. Nothing like that here.'

There was a twinkle in his eye. Perhaps he really did understand what it meant to her, working somewhere like this. She had more time for him too, which had to be a definite bonus.

'Is there any social life here?' he went on.

'There's a cinema and a theatre,' she

replied, brightening. 'Why, Pa, do you fancy seeing a film or something?'

'No, not me,' he said. 'You! It's no good you sitting in here with me every night. Why don't you go out a bit, have some fun?'

'Pa, I don't want to go out. I'm quite happy to spend my evenings here with you,' she told him firmly. 'But if you fancy seeing a film, I'll come with you. I happen to know that there's a ramp at the cinema and the theatre. In fact, most places here cater for wheelchairs.'

'I don't want to go out,' he said huffily, breaking off a chunk of bread. 'I don't want people staring at me, looking and talking.'

'But no one here knows you, Pa.'

'They'll look at me with pity in their eyes and I can't stand that, Kate.'

'Then prove to them that you don't need their pity,' she challenged him.

'No,' he said shortly. 'Isn't it about time you were getting back to your patients?'

She'd been dismissed. Sometimes he

could be so cruel without even realising it. Didn't he know how much she loved him; how she worried about him? She got up and took their empty bowls out to the kitchen.

'He's got a real cob on today,' Mrs Mayes said.

'He's depressed,' Kate said softly. 'Perhaps I could ask one of the other doctors to call and see him. Geoffrey Blair is the geriatric expert.'

'Don't let your father hear you say that!' Mrs Mayes cried. 'He wouldn't like you calling him geriatric. Come to that, neither do I. He's not that much older than me.'

Mrs Mayes put up a pretence of being offended that made Kate smile before she continued. 'Dr Blair has had a lot of experience with stroke victims who have to deal with similar feelings. His wife, Denise, is the physiotherapist at the hospital and they work as a team. He's also a lovely man.'

'Well, you must do whatever you think best,' Mrs Mayes said. 'I offered to push him into the town this morning as it's such a lovely day, but he wouldn't hear of it.'

When Kate returned to the living room, her father had moved his wheelchair back to the window. 'I've got to go now, Pa,' she said, stooping to drop a kiss on his forehead. 'I may be a little late home this evening. Dr Lawrence wants to talk to me about something.'

He didn't answer again, and she felt her heart sink. As she was about to leave, he called her back. 'Kate.'

'Pa?'

'It's not just my stupid pride,' he said thickly. 'It's you.'

'Me?'

He turned his head slightly so he could look at her, and she could hardly bear to see the pain in his eyes. 'This isn't the life I'd planned for you, or the life you'd planned for yourself. If it wasn't for me you'd be married by now, probably with a baby or two.'

'That's nonsense, Pa,' she said.

'Is it?'

'You know it is,' she said and kissed him again. 'Have to go.'

'Take care,' he said as she was leaving.

As usual when she left the house, she tried to put worries about her father to the back of her mind. Now she looked ahead and wondered what Cory wanted to discuss with her.

3

'Did you enjoy your lunch?' Cory appeared from nowhere as Kate walked into the clinic, making her jump.

'Do you have to do that?' she cried. 'Creeping up on people. What on earth are you playing at?'

'I'm not playing at anything, Kate,' he replied, frowning in concern. 'It's not right that you're so jumpy. You're safe here.'

Kate breathed in slowly, gently exhaling until she felt steady again. She'd never get used to not having to be afraid; never. At last she felt able to speak again. 'You can't afford to be complacent wherever you happen to live. There are drugs in the pharmacy, remember.'

'That's very true, Kate. I'm sorry if I alarmed you, but I promise you, I'm not in the least complacent about the possible hazards. I won't let anything happen to you,' he said, his voice gentle.

What did he mean, he wouldn't let anything happen to her? She wasn't his responsibility. Shaking her head, she made her way to her room and prepared for her first patient.

During afternoon surgery, Kate was called to the hospital to attend an emergency admission. With a brief apology to her waiting patients, she hurried through the connecting doors from the clinic to the hospital. They didn't have an accident and emergency department as such, but the practice nurse, Barbara Leon, generally dealt with emergency admissions as well as running her own clinics.

'Adam Sneddon is two years old,' Barbara explained as Kate entered the treatment room. 'He was running around when he slipped and fell, knocking his head on the corner of an inside wall.'

'Right, thanks, Barbara. Let's have a look, shall we?'

Kate stepped into one of the two cubicles in the treatment room and at once saw that the mother was far more upset than the child. She looked close to tears and was clutching her little boy's hand. In a steel dish were several large pads of blood-soaked cotton wool. The child was lying on his back. He was pale, but seemed more interested in the cartoon posters on the ceiling than the wound in the centre of his forehead.

'Hello,' Kate said. 'I'm Dr Ross. Could you tell me how this happened?'

Mrs Sneddon repeated what Barbara Leon had already told her as Kate quickly examined the little boy. He even managed a little smile when she shone her torch into his eyes.

'Did he lose consciousness at all?'

'I don't think so. I mean, he started to scream almost immediately.'

'Good.' Kate smiled. 'Any vomiting?'

'No. I didn't know what to do,

Doctor. I just soaked a pad of cotton wool with cold water and held it to his head. There was blood everywhere. You can see from the state of his T-shirt. I jumped in the car and drove straight here.'

'You did the right thing,' Kate said reassuringly. 'I'm going to have to put a few stitches in there though.'

'Will he have a scar?'

'There will be a slight scar there,' she said. 'But I'll do my very best to make sure it's small.' She now turned her attention back to the little boy.

'Will you wait outside please, Mrs Sneddon?' Nurse Leon said briskly, taking the anxious mother by the arm. 'You can have a seat in the waiting area.'

'Do I have to?' Mrs Sneddon said, panic-stricken at the thought of being parted from her child. Kate shot Barbara a look.

'You're welcome to stay with Adam,' Kate said. 'Perhaps you'd like to hold his hand.'

'So long as she doesn't faint.' Barbara muttered.

'Mrs Sneddon won't faint, will you?' Kate said cheerfully. She hoped she hadn't offended Barbara, but in her experience children were far better in this sort of situation with a parent present. And besides, Mrs Sneddon had coped well so far. If she were likely to faint or go to pieces, she would have done so by now.

Adam didn't flinch as Kate injected local anaesthetic around the edges of the wound. 'Good boy,' she said softly. Then she smiled at his mum who was watching, enthralled as Kate worked. 'All right, Mrs Sneddon?'

The tension in the woman's face relaxed a little, soothed by Kate's gentle smile, and she nodded.

'Won't be very much longer.'

He lay perfectly still, like a little angel, while she put four small, neat sutures into his forehead. When she'd finished, she stepped back to admire her handiwork.

'Lovely job, Doctor,' Barbara remarked. 'Very neat. There'll hardly be a mark there at all.'

'Thank you,' Kate said with a smile. 'I couldn't have done it if Adam hadn't been so good. Have we a sticker we can give him for being a brave boy?'

'Certainly.' Barbara smiled and produced a large, round sticker proclaiming I WAS BRAVE, which she stuck firmly to the front of Adam's bloodstained T-shirt.

When Mrs Sneddon and Adam had gone, Barbara cleaned up in the cubicle. 'What a sweet little boy,' Kate remarked. 'If only all our patients were as cooperative as him.'

'That age, they're no problem,' Barbara replied. 'We've had children in here — big children — and they've made much more fuss than that. But it's the adults, especially men, who are the biggest babies.'

'I won't argue with that.' Kate laughed. 'Barbara, about earlier . . . '

'Mothers can be a real pain at times.' Barbara smiled, knowing exactly what

Kate was going to say. 'When it's their child lying there hurting they turn into lionesses, determined to protect their offspring at all costs. Last year an anxious mother gave me a black eye and I've been a bit cautious ever since.'

'Really?' Kate gasped. 'Here?'

'Yes, here.' Barbara's smile became rueful. 'She was mortified afterwards and I decided not to press charges, but it was pretty scary at the time, I'm telling you.'

'I can imagine,' Kate said. 'As long as there are no hard feelings?'

'No, forget it,' Barbara replied. 'I don't offend easily, I promise you. See this skin? It's as thick as the hide of a rhinoceros.'

Kate found that hard to believe looking at the perfect clear, creamy skin of the beautiful nurse. 'I'd better be getting back. I've several patients waiting. See you later, Barbara.'

'Doctor Lawrence has seen the rest of your patients,' Gaynor told Kate on her return to the clinic reception. 'He asked me to send you straight to his office when he returned.'

Instead of being pleased, Kate was fuming. How dare he take over her surgery? She hadn't been gone that long.

She marched down the corridor to his room and knocked sharply on the door, waiting for him to say 'come in' before pushing the door open. 'What do you mean by taking over my surgery?' she said.

'I beg your pardon?'

'My patients.'

He sat up straight and looked her in the eye. 'Sit down, Kate,' he said. It wasn't a request. Kate sat. 'I don't know how you did things at your last place of work, but obviously we do things differently here. If one of the doctors is called out on an emergency, the rest of us take any patients who are waiting. Of course any who specifically want to see the doctor who has been called away are entitled to wait or make another appointment. Your patients were given the choice and were all quite happy to see myself and Dr Blair.'

'I see,' she said softly, feeling foolish and not really knowing why she'd blown up like that. 'I'm sorry, Dr Lawrence.' Normally they were on first-name terms, but as he was giving her a ticking-off, she felt under the circumstances it wouldn't be right.

'You were seeing to a child with a head injury, I understand.'

'That's right.'

'Everything satisfactory?'

'Perfectly.'

'Good. My other reason for wanting to get your patients out of the way was so that I could talk to you. Can you spare a couple of minutes?' He smiled. He was so nice!

'Of course,' she said. She really wished she didn't have to be so cool towards him, but her father needed her right now and would go on needing her for the rest of his life. She wouldn't abandon him, nor would she expect any man to have to share her burden. She'd learned that lesson early on. Gareth, her fiancé at the time of her parents' accident, had called off their engagement almost immediately. As soon as he realised Kate's father would be dependent upon her, he'd got out of the relationship.

And it had been the same story ever since. Every time a man became even remotely interested in her, once he found out about her father he'd back off. She didn't blame them. If it was a child she was tied to, there was always the possibility of the child eventually leaving home, but her father was a lifelong commitment.

'Before you joined us, we were already looking at new ways of serving the community. One thing I think would be useful would be to hold a rather more comprehensive well-woman clinic. And that's where you come in, Kate.'

Kate shifted uncomfortably when she remembered something Barbara had said when she first joined the team: 'So you're the token woman.' That was it. Kate couldn't think what she'd meant by that remark.

'Would you be prepared to take on a regular clinic, Kate? You'd be seeing all patients, not just your own, and covering all the usual — breast checks, cervical screening and so on.' She pressed her lips together and he looked baffled. 'Now what have I said?'

'Of course I'd be willing,' she began. 'But tell me, did I get the job here because I'm a woman and that suited your plans, or because you wanted a doctor to double up as a second practice nurse? Surely screening patients is Barbara's area.'

'You were offered the post here because of your excellent qualifications,' he said. 'We also needed an anaesthetist, which you are. You ticked all our boxes, Kate.'

'I see.'

'And Barbara has her hands full with her clinics. We could afford to take on an extra GP or another practice nurse and we decided on you. I'm sorry if I've offended you. I had no idea I was taking on a rampant feminist.'

'A what?' Kate cried. 'You couldn't be more wrong. Is this because I turned you down earlier?'

'Turned me down? Oh, you mean the theatre group. It's no big deal. It's just that I've noticed you don't appear to have any kind of a social life. I was just trying to make you feel welcome here, that's all.'

She felt so confused and embarrassed that she hardly knew whether she was coming or going, and what he said next made her feel even worse.

'I can't promise not to ask you out again though. When I interviewed you for the position here, you led me to believe you were eager to become a part of the community. It's vital here. Were you deliberately misleading me to secure the job?'

'No, I didn't intend to mislead you. It's just proving more difficult than I thought it would be.'

'It doesn't have to be difficult,' he said sympathetically. 'Anyway, I thought alternate Wednesday afternoons for the clinic to begin with, until we see how much of a success it is. Would that suit you?'

She nodded, not trusting herself to speak.

'Good.'

'Will that be all?'

'For now,' he said. 'Perhaps you could have a word with Gaynor on your way out. She's rather artistic and I'm sure she'd love to design a poster advertising the new service.'

Smiling despite herself, she said, 'Goodbye, Cory.'

'That's better.' He grinned. 'Have a good evening, and I'll see you tomorrow. And Kate . . . '

'Yes?'

'You don't have to be afraid.'

'I know,' she murmured.

4

Kate hurried back to reception, where she found Gaynor in conversation with Barbara.

Barbara turned as Kate approached, and smiled. 'Another one ready for home,' she said cheerily. 'Are you feeling all right, Kate? You look terribly flushed.'

'I'm fine,' Kate muttered. 'I've been rushing, that's all.'

'Well, that's me done for today,' Barbara went on. 'Night, Kate. Night, Gaynor. See you tomorrow.'

'Bye, Barbara,' Gaynor said. 'Have a good time tonight.'

'Oh, I will,' Barbara laughed.

'Going somewhere nice?' Kate asked.

'I'm going to see the theatre group's latest offering,' Barbara said with a beaming smile. 'Thanks to Cory.'

Kate felt as if she'd been thumped.

She turned and stared out after Barbara's retreating figure, feeling a terrible pang of jealousy.

She felt a light touch on her arm and spun round to find Gaynor looking at her. 'Kate, did you want me for something?'

'Oh, Gaynor, yes. Cory says you're artistic. Do you think you could do me a poster advertising my new well-woman clinic? I'll be holding it on alternate Wednesday afternoons, usual surgery hours.'

'Will do,' Gaynor said.

With a huge sigh of relief, Kate hurried from the building.

* * *

Kate walked into the clinic the next morning and found the reception area buzzing with staff. In the centre of it all stood Barbara, her laughter light and frothy, bubbling above the general hubbub.

'We just cracked up,' Barbara said.

'First the lights kept flashing on and off, then dear old Betty Roberts forgot her lines. It was absolute mayhem, but extremely entertaining.'

Kate smiled and tried to push her way through, but somehow she was drawn into the small crowd and forced to listen to Barbara's account of the events of the previous night. It was ridiculous that she should feel so put out. She'd had the chance to go to the theatre with Cory and she'd turned him down. What did she expect him to do? Sit at home on his own letting two perfectly good tickets go to waste?

'We had a lovely meal at the Waterside Hotel afterwards,' Barbara went on. 'The new chef there is everything he's cracked up to be.'

A meal afterwards. Kate couldn't remember the last time she'd been out for a meal.

'And the company of course was divine,' Barbara went on. 'So romantic.' This brought a fresh torrent of questions.

'Excuse me,' Kate said, this time determined to push her way through. Hurrying down towards her surgery, she could hear the laughter following her and her cheeks burned.

'Kate.' Cory came out of his surgery and almost crashed right into her. Instinctively reaching out, he steadied her and at the same time managed to look deep into her eyes. 'Is something wrong? You seem upset.'

'My father,' she began, but didn't quite know where to go next, or what to say. What could she say? Where her father was concerned, she just felt so utterly helpless.

'Is he ill?' Cory asked at once. Gales of laughter drifted towards them and Cory looked up impatiently. 'Look, come in here for a minute. It's quieter.' She hesitated and he added, 'It may help to talk.' He put his hand on her waist and pushed her gently into his surgery, then motioning to a chair said, 'Sit.'

Kate sank into the chair and felt

absurdly close to tears. She'd been awake most of the night worrying, and even when it came, sleep had presented no solution. Looking up, she saw that Cory was watching her closely, lines of concern running across his forehead. He seemed to be waiting for her to say something, but she didn't know where to start.

Cory turned to his computer and keyed in his password. Seconds later, everything he needed to know about David Ross was on screen. For a few moments he read in silence. Then he turned to Kate, his expression sombre. 'You mentioned none of this to me, Kate,' he said. 'Why?'

'Personal . . . '

'Kate, your father should be receiving treatment. Regular physiotherapy at least.'

'Do you think I don't know that?' Kate said. 'He's my father and he used to be a doctor. Not some patient who will meekly do as he's told. I've tried to persuade him to come to the hospital, but he won't budge from the bungalow. He sits in that wretched wheelchair day after day, hour after hour, gazing out at the sea. He's got no motivation, no will. He may as well have died along with my mother for all the sense his life makes right now.' Her own words startled and frightened her and she clapped her hand to her mouth and stared at Cory, white-faced with shock. How could she have said that? What on earth had possessed her?

'I think I should come out to the bungalow and introduce myself to your father, don't you?' Cory said with a gentle smile. 'I'll have to have a word with Geoffrey and find out why he hasn't been to see your father himself. He should have familiarised himself with these notes by now.'

'Don't blame Geoffrey,' Kate said softly. 'Pa won't accept help of any kind, no matter how it's wrapped up.'

'Is that why you went into general practice, Kate?'

'It was easier, yes,' she admitted reluctantly.

'Is he aware of that?'

'He's aware of everything,' she answered ruefully. 'The thing is, Cory, I'm glad I made the change when I did. I enjoy general practice, I really do, but of course he doesn't believe me.'

'Yes,' Cory smiled warmly. 'I can imagine. You must get that stubborn streak from him. Now, stop worrying about him, Kate, and that's an order.'

Oh, if only it could be that easy, Kate thought. But somehow she felt better having finally spoken to Cory.

'Why don't you ask me over for dinner one evening,' he suggested. 'We could make it an informal visit so as not to put him under any undue pressure. And as he's not registered with me but with Geoffrey, he wouldn't suspect anything.'

'He's fairly astute, my father.' Kate grinned. 'It won't be easy to put one over on him.'

'We could pretend that my interest is

in you,' he said, sitting back with a wicked grin that made her heart flip.

'All right.' She smiled at last. 'If you're sure you don't mind?'

'Mind?' He laughed. 'It'll be a pleasure. How about Monday?'

'Monday. So soon,' she gasped.

'Monday it is then. That's Gaynor buzzing to let me know my first patient is here.'

Kate stood up quickly, thanked him and hurried to her own surgery. The waiting room at the end of the corridor was already beginning to fill up. It was going to be a busy morning.

Kate was on her way to her first home visit when her mobile phone rang. She pulled to the side of the road to answer the call.

'Can you go to Cliff House? It's right at the top of the cliff in a terrace of about a dozen,' Gaynor said urgently. 'John Harris called to say he thinks his wife is having a heart attack. She's breathless and has chest pains. Her name's Anne and she's thirty-three years old. I haven't called out an ambulance, but I've got one standing by.'

'Thanks, Gaynor. I'm on my way,' Kate responded and immediately squeezed on the accelerator pedal. Her own heart began to race. A thirty-three-year-old woman was an unlikely heart attack candidate, but there were exceptions to every rule.

She pulled up outside the tall terraced house and almost at once, the front door flew open and a young, worried-looking man rushed out to meet her. 'Dr Ross? Thank goodness you're here.'

Grabbing her bag, she hurried up the steps and into the house.

'I'm not having a heart attack. I'm just tired, that's all. Why did you have to call out the doctor? It's a waste of time.' She broke off and clenched her teeth.

'Pain?' Kate asked as she knelt down on the floor beside the sofa.

'In my chest. But it's not as bad as

John makes out. It's very slight and I can't seem to get my breath. I usually only get it when I've been running or hurrying.'

'Usually?' Kate's eyebrows rose.

'Shouldn't you be giving her heart massage or something?' John Harris said. He was pacing up and down like a nervous father-to-be.

'I get out of breath easily,' Anne went on. 'And I feel so tired all the time. I feel . . . ' She sighed. 'I feel so down, Doctor. I've constantly got a mouth full of ulcers, so I can't eat properly.'

'She won't come to the clinic,' John said. 'That's why I called you out, Doctor. Desperation.'

Kate nodded and popped a thermometer into Anne's mouth while she took her pulse. 'You're certainly very pale, but you're not having a heart attack,' she said gently. 'I'll just check your blood pressure. Mr Harris, why don't you go and make a cup of tea? There's really nothing to worry about.'

When he'd gone, Kate asked, 'How

long have you been feeling like this?'

'Forever,' Anne said, her voice cracking. 'It feels like it anyway. I've got no energy.'

Kate asked questions and made notes, waiting until she'd got the full picture before gently checking Anne's inner eyelids. They were so pale as to be almost bloodless. It was an unreliable test, but as far as Kate was concerned, it confirmed her diagnosis.

'I'm going to take a little blood for testing,' she said, searching through her bag for a syringe and a haematology envelope. 'I'm ninety-nine percent sure it will confirm that you're anaemic.'

'What's happening?' John returned carrying a tray which had obviously been hastily laid. 'Why are you sitting like that?'

'I just had a blood test,' Anne said. 'Do stop worrying, John. The doctor thinks I'm just anaemic, that's all.'

'Phew, well that's better than a heart attack. Sorry I went off at the deep end. Tea for you, Doctor?'

'No, thanks,' Kate said, quickly looking at her watch. 'I've a number of house calls still to make and I ought to be on my way. I will make you an appointment for next Wednesday afternoon. I'm holding a well-woman clinic and I'd like to see you there.'

Kate hurried out of the house and down the steps and for the second time that day cannoned straight into Cory Lawrence. He grabbed her, stopped her falling over and laughed softly. 'Steady on, Kate. I was coming up this way to see a patient and I thought you might find Anne Harris's notes helpful.' Smiling, he handed her a brown envelope. Hands shaking, Kate took it. Then he had turned around and was hurrying away. She watched him go, a curious tightness in her chest.

5

That evening as Kate was about to leave her office, the telephone on her desk buzzed. 'Could you come in for a minute, Kate?' Before she could reply, the phone had been put down again.

With a puzzled frown, she picked up her bag and went across to Cory's room and knocked on the door.

'Come in, Kate.' He looked up at her and grinned. She sank nervously onto the chair and clasped her hands together on her lap.

'I've been thinking about your father,' he said. 'We ought to get our heads together over this before Monday, to sort out some sort of action plan.'

'Oh, I don't think that's necessary,' she began.

'You do want to help your father, don't you?'

'Of course I do.'

'Then we'll have lunch tomorrow. My house. Shall we say one o'clock? Good.'

Once again, Kate felt as if she'd been run over by a steamroller. Yet it was done in the nicest way. And he was only inviting her for lunch for heaven's sake — but at his house.

There was a knock on the door and he said, 'I'll see you tomorrow then, Kate. Don't forget to tell your father you're coming. It's all part of my cunning plan.'

She stood up and opened the door and found herself face to face with Barbara. 'Hello, Kate,' Barbara said chirpily. Coming right into the room, she went over to the desk. 'And hello, you.' Her voice was loaded with affection. 'Did I ever tell you what a wonderful man you are?'

'No, I don't think so,' Cory chuckled warmly. 'But feel free to do so.'

'About last night,' Barbara went on. 'I had a wonderful time.'

Head bowed, Kate rushed through

the door and closed it behind her.

Driving home was a pleasure. No one rushed along these narrow roads, and another driver was more likely to wave you through than rush to jump in front of you. Life here was far easier on her clutch and her brake pads than city life had been. It was like living in a different world entirely.

It was a lovely light evening and Mrs Mayes had pushed David Ross out onto the veranda where he sat, a blanket over his knees, gazing out towards the distant horizon.

Kate felt that familiar surge of love and affection well up inside her at the sight of him. He'd been such a tower of strength during her life; it still felt strange to see him looking so helpless and vulnerable — this man who used to ride her on his shoulders and run whooping down hills until she screamed with fright and excitement.

'Hello, Pa,' she said, joining him. 'Are you warm enough out here? It feels a bit chilly.'

'Does it?' he answered dully so that her heart twisted with grief and pain.

'Come on, I'll take you inside and tell you all my news.' He brightened a little at the happy lilt in her voice.

'Ah, you're home.' Mrs Mayes appeared. 'I thought I heard the car. I'll get the dinner on if that's all right, Dr Ross.'

'Yes, thank you, Mrs Mayes.'

'What's your news?' David asked.

'Well, first I'm going to hold a regular well-woman clinic at the health centre,' she said.

'Isn't that handled by the practice nurse?'

'Normally, yes,' Kate said. 'But also, Dr Lawrence — Cory has invited me to his house for lunch tomorrow.'

This time her father's joy was obvious. His face cracked into a smile and something that looked very much like relief flooded his features. 'This Dr Lawrence,' he said at last, his voice carefully controlled. 'Good-looking, is he?'

Kate blushed. It wouldn't be difficult convincing her father that there was a romantic interest at the heart of all this, because in her case it wasn't that far from the truth. It would just come down to how good an actor Cory was.

'So he's good-looking,' he said without waiting for her reply. 'And a good doctor?'

'Very good, Pa,' Kate said emphatically. 'In fact, he reminds me of you.'

'Ah, a doctor of the old school.' David nodded approvingly.

'But with his finger on the pulse so he knows what's happening here and now,' Kate added. 'Exactly like you.'

'You really like him, don't you?' David said. 'I hope he's worth it, my love. You've been hurt so many times.'

'Oh, Pa.' Kate turned away.

'Why don't you ask him for dinner one evening next week?' he suggested.

It was all Kate could do to keep herself from bursting out laughing. This was working better than she could have dreamed. Cory had been right. 'You wouldn't mind?' she asked, her mouth twitching on a smile.

'Kate, all I want is to see you happy and settled. You can't imagine how it makes me feel seeing you sitting here night after night when you could be out having a good time.'

Kate squeezed his hand. 'Pa, I love you and I love being with you.'

'I love you, too,' he said. 'But I miss your mother so much at times; it's like an ache inside. Do you see what I'm saying to you, Kate?'

'I think so.' She nodded. 'I'll ask him for dinner, then.'

Mrs Mayes was thrilled when David told her that they were to have a dinner guest. 'It'll probably be Monday,' Kate said. 'I know that's a good night for him.'

'That's the other doctor,' Mrs Mayes said, frowning. 'The younger one. I thought Dr Blair was . . . '

Kate shot her a look and she clamped her lips together. But she needn't have worried. Her father was so delighted with her having apparently made a friend, he hadn't caught on.

'No, Mrs Mayes,' he said. 'I'm registered with Dr Blair. Dr Lawrence isn't coming here to see me, but to see Kate. Isn't that right, Kate?'

Mrs Mayes looked at Kate, her sharp eyes missing nothing. *Please don't say anything*, Kate thought, willing the housekeeper not to give her away. 'That's right, Pa,' she said at last. 'Will that be all right with you, Mrs Mayes?'

'Monday? Fine.' Mrs Mayes smiled broadly and Kate felt the tension flood from her body. 'Monday,' she went on thoughtfully. 'I'll do a salad, I think. And a cheese and broccoli flan. Would that be all right, Dr Ross?'

Bless her heart. Mrs Mayes had thought of the kind of meal most easily managed by her father. She smiled a special smile at Kate that warmed her heart. 'That would be perfect, Mrs Mayes,' she said.

Beatrice Mayes met her eyes with a smile. 'Don't you think it's about time you started calling me Bea?' she asked.

'Bea.' Kate smiled. 'And I'm Kate from now on.'

David clicked his tongue and both women laughed. 'If his lordship had his way, I'd curtsey every time I came into the room,' Bea said with a grin, and to Kate's amazement her father chuckled.

'Know your place, woman,' he said, and just when Kate would have scolded him for being so rude, Bea burst out laughing.

The following morning, Kate was woken by the telephone.

'Kate, can you come to the hospital straight away?' It was Cory and it sounded urgent.

She was already sitting up on the edge of her bed. 'Of course. What is it?'

'I need an anaesthetist,' he said. 'I'm about to take a patient to the hospital for an emergency appendectomy. We can't get an ambulance here to take him to the General, so if you could meet me in theatre that would be great.'

'I'm on my way,' Kate said.

Within five minutes she was leaving the house and driving through the empty roads towards the hospital. She arrived as Cory ran through the doors with the little boy in his arms. His face was flushed deep red, but around his eyes and mouth his skin was deathly pale. He was barely conscious, and moaning in pain.

His mother looked shell-shocked. 'I thought it was just a tummy bug,' she kept repeating, over and over. 'Poor little mite. He's in agony.'

'I'm Dr Ross,' Kate introduced herself quickly. 'I need to ask you some questions about..?'

'Daniel. His name's Daniel,' the woman said, watching as Cory spirited her son away.

'About Daniel,' Kate went on. Someone handed her a form on a clipboard and she looked up gratefully to see it was Barbara. 'Thanks,' she said before turning back to the boy's mother and taking the necessary notes.

Within minutes, Kate was in the small operating theatre, the little boy was under, and Cory was concentrating deeply on the job in hand, assisted very ably by Barbara. From her position beside Daniel's head, Kate couldn't see how the operation was going and had to rely on the conversation taking place between Cory and Barbara.

Kate heard an instrument hit a steel dish. 'Look at the size of that.'

'Ooh, that baby was ready to blow,' Barbara said incredulously.

'How's he doing, Kate?'

'Steady,' Kate replied. 'All good.'

How well Cory and Barbara worked together, Kate thought. As if they'd been doing it for years. They probably had. Barbara was that most valuable of nurses who seemed to anticipate the doctor's needs in advance. She often passed things to Cory before he even asked for them and when she did, his eyes would crinkle above his mask as he smiled.

There was much more than a

professional relationship there, Kate decided. Some kind of chemistry was at work between those two. How silly she'd been to think that he'd have a romantic interest in her when his heart clearly lay elsewhere.

Afterwards, the three of them sat drinking coffee. For the first time, Kate looked properly at Cory. The stubble on his face was darker than ever and his eyes looked tired and heavy. Even looking like that, he was still incredibly attractive. He looked up, caught her staring and grinned, his ready smile making her heart leap.

'I know what you're thinking,' he said.

For a moment it was as if there was just the two of them in the room. Kate had never been as aware of her own heartbeat as she was now. She felt her cheeks burn and her throat constricted as she tried to speak. Glancing at Barbara, she realised the nurse was watching her closely.

'Do you?'

He rasped his hand across his chin. 'You're thinking I need a shave,' he said.

'Yes,' she laughed, relieved. 'That's exactly what I was thinking.'

'Really, Dr Ross,' Barbara said stiffly. 'You may have taken the time to make yourself look presentable, but Dr Lawrence has different priorities.'

Kate's eyes widened. 'But I . . . ' What was the use? All she'd done to make herself look presentable, as Barbara put it, was to run a brush through her hair and splash her face with cold water. Her priorities had been the same as Cory's, to get to the hospital as speedily as possible.

'Kate got here as quickly as she could,' Cory said in her defence before draining his cup. 'But you're right, Kate. I do need to tidy up. If you'll excuse me, ladies.'

'He's been on duty all night,' Barbara said when he'd gone. 'Can't you cut the guy some slack?'

'I didn't mean any criticism,' Kate

said defensively. Barbara put her hand to her forehead and squeezed her eyes shut.

'I'm sorry, Kate,' she said. 'I guess we're all tired. I shouldn't take it out on you.'

Bewildered, Kate said, 'I'm sorry, too, Barbara.'

'We're running a well-woman clinic next Wednesday, I understand,' Barbara went on. 'About time, too, if you ask me.'

'It's your idea?'

'No! It's been a dream of Cory's for some time. After all, as he says, it's their health service, so they're entitled to the best they can get from it.'

'Well,' Kate said, getting to her feet. 'I'd better get back home and get cleaned up myself.'

'I'm sorry about what I said earlier,' Barbara said, also standing up. 'You always appear so calm and unruffled, even when you've been woken so early. How do you do it?'

'It's the haircut,' Kate laughed. 'It's

so short, a quick brush and it looks tidy.'

Barbara patted her own neat pleat of hair. It was jet-black and shone like a raven's wing. 'I'd like mine short for the convenience,' she remarked. 'But men — well, my man.' She gave Kate a smile. 'He likes it long.'

Kate's throat felt tight. Her man. Cory?

'Cory's right about you, Kate,' Barbara said, her voice kind. 'You need to make friends here. You seem . . . I don't know, sort of cut off from the rest of us.'

Kate recoiled, shaken. So he had been discussing her with Barbara of all people. Mumbling an excuse, she fled from the day room and out to her car. Home — she had to get home, back on familiar ground. But just as she was beginning to feel better, a voice called to her across the car park. She spun round.

'Is that better?' Cory leaned forward, offering his chin for inspection. It looked smooth now, but still rugged. It was a large, square chin, a sign of strength Kate always felt.

'Better?' she breathed angrily. 'How dare you?'

'What have I done now?' he said, looking genuinely puzzled.

'How dare you discuss me with Barbara Leon? I suppose you told her all about my father, too.'

'I've told her nothing,' he said. 'Why on earth would I discuss you or your father with her?'

'Well I don't know!' Kate cried.

'For goodness sake, Kate, I wish you'd realise that we all care about each other here and now you're part of the team, that includes you whether you like it or not.' With that, he turned on his heel and strode back towards the hospital.

What on earth is wrong with me? she thought. Moving house, changing jobs, taking care of an invalid parent all scored pretty high on the stress-o-meter, but Kate had never had any problem coping before. She'd been mugged at knifepoint for heaven's sake. If it hadn't been for the timely arrival of someone else, goodness knew what could have happened. She'd even been held hostage briefly in a damp, mould-ridden flat by a man with a toy gun. Yes, she'd been ninety percent sure that he wouldn't harm her, but he was desperate. His three children were all asthmatics and the damp and mould exacerbated the condition. Finding cockroaches in his baby daughter's cot had been the last straw.

There was none of that at Wyatt's Cove. No grinding poverty, no real danger. It was safe — a haven from the cruel outside world.

She took one last look at the hospital and saw him standing at the window of the ward where their little patient was now recovering. He was staring down at her, but from this distance it was impossible to read his expression. Kate stared back at him, transfixed. Then she saw Barbara appear at his side and as she watched, the venetian blind slid down and the slats were closed, shutting her out.

Kate got into her car and headed home for breakfast with her father.

6

'I'm off now, Kate. You haven't forgotten lunch?'

Kate looked up. It was the first time she'd seen Cory since early that morning. She'd already decided not to go to his house for lunch, feeling sure she wouldn't be welcome.

'Sure you still want me to come?' she asked tentatively.

'Why shouldn't I?' he asked. 'Because we had words this morning?' Without waiting for her answer he went on, 'Can you find your way there? It's on the north cliff. Looks like a log cabin. You've probably passed it a few times.'

'Yes, I know it,' she replied.

'I'll see you later then.' With a dazzling smile, he was gone.

She still had nearly an hour before she had to leave the clinic, and planned to spend the time catching up on her correspondence and reports. But Kate was glad of the work, for it helped take her mind off Cory and their lunch date.

It's not really a date, she mused. *More of an arrangement to discuss how best to treat my father, without him realising.* Therapy could help him so much; he knew that as well as she did. The truth was, he just didn't want to get any better. He was waiting to die: that was the bare truth of it.

When it was time for her to leave, Kate was feeling decidedly shaky. Her knees felt weak and trembly and her hands were sweaty. She put it down to hunger. She took her time driving to his house and when she reached it, she sat outside in her car on the sloping drive. It did look like a log cabin, of Scandinavian design with an A-frame. Through the vertical blinds at the windows, she could see large green plants growing in big tubs and felt a tickling at her curiosity.

She climbed out of the car and realised she was running late. Exuding a confidence she didn't feel, she walked briskly to the front door and knocked. Surely he hadn't forgotten she was coming, she thought when he still hadn't answered after her third knock.

Like her house, Cory's was surrounded by a veranda. She walked around the deck to the back and was surprised to find another level to the house below her feet. So it appeared to be just a small log cabin when in fact another floor was hidden down below — and she was standing on its roof. How very odd. She leaned on the rail and looked out to sea, enjoying the feel of the wind in her face.

Down below she could see the beach. Then she spotted a figure on the shore, strolling along at the water's edge with a dog. Even at this distance she could see the dog was a border collie just from the way she was trying to round up the seabirds. Shielding her eyes from the sun, Kate peered down and realised it was Cory. He was wearing black trousers and a black jumper, and every so often would throw a ball for the dog to chase. Obviously he'd decided when she was late that she wasn't going to show up at all.

She was starving. She'd had no appetite for breakfast and she'd been up since Cory had called her to the hospital first thing. Her stomach growled and with a determined step she made her way towards the steps, which would take her all the way down to the beach.

The sand was soft and dry and the high heels on her shoes wrung her feet over. She reached down and pulled them off, feeling the softness of the sand beneath her feet. It felt curiously soothing and she realised it was her first visit to the beach since she'd come here.

Magically, the tension and anger began to recede, lulled by the soft warmth of the sand and the gentle motion of the sea as it rustled through the shingle at the water's edge.

Cory was walking away from her.

Where on earth was he going? She hurried along the sand, her feet sinking and slipping, the muscles in her legs protesting at this unusual strain. At last, when she guessed he was in hearing range, she called his name.

He turned at once. The dog saw her at the same time and came splashing out of the sea in a crest of white foam. It gave a joyful shrill bark and began to race towards her as if she were an old, long-lost friend.

'No!' Cory yelled. 'Molly, no! Stop! Don't jump up!'

But Molly was determined. As she ran towards Kate, she could see droplets of water flying in all directions.

'Molly!' Cory's voice was authoritative, but Molly couldn't have cared less. Kate stood her ground, bracing herself. She knew she had nothing to fear from the dog except maybe torn tights and a soaking. Cory broke into a run, still shouting at the dog.

Seconds before Molly hit, Kate closed her eyes. She felt a sodden,

sandy thud against her legs. Then the dog was rolling on her back, kicking her legs in the air and wagging her tail like mad. Laughing, Kate crouched down and tickled Molly's sandy tummy.

'Bad girl,' Cory growled when he finally arrived, but his voice carried no conviction. 'I'm so sorry about this, Kate. She has absolutely no manners at all.'

'She's gorgeous,' Kate said.

'Mad you mean,' he laughed. 'But I wouldn't change her for the world.'

'Good for you,' Kate said and straightened up. But Molly wanted more and shuffled along on her bottom until she was almost sitting on Kate's feet, her head pressed against Kate's legs. She couldn't have got any closer. When Kate tried to ignore her, she lifted a paw and dragged it down Kate's leg, snagging her tights.

This time there was no doubting the anger in Cory's voice. 'Bad girl, Molly.' She looked sheepish but not cowed, and backed away to sit, her tail still

swishing furiously from side to side on the sand, a laugh on her sandy face.

'Shall we walk back?'

Kate fell into step beside him with Molly running ahead, and after a while Cory stopped and looked down at her. 'I had no idea I was working with someone so vertically challenged,' he said with a wry grin.

Kate forgot why she was here. She even forgot about her father and her responsibilities. 'Vertically challenged?' She hit out at him with her shoes and missed as he ran out of reach. 'You won't get away with that,' she called, breaking into a run.

Molly joined in the chase, barking shrilly as Kate tried again and again to catch Cory and punish him. She'd always been ribbed about her height — or lack of it. The chase went on until laughter and lack of breath stopped Kate in her tracks. She bent double, resting her hands on her thighs, gulping in huge breaths of air. 'Now see what you've done,' she panted. 'I've got a stitch.'

'A stitch.' Cory bellowed with laughter. 'I haven't heard that expression for years.'

The laughter was good. Kate joined in, letting herself go for the first time in goodness knew how long. It only stopped when Cory looked at his watch and exclaimed, 'It's stopped. What's the time, Kate?'

'Half past one,' she said, sobering quickly from the drunken effect of the laughter.

'Oh no. Lunch will be burned.'

'Never mind,' she said, starting to run ahead of him up the steps. 'Perhaps we can rescue it. What was it?'

With a perfectly steady voice he said, 'Salad.'

She stopped, turned to face him and found herself on his eye level. The breath caught in her throat and stopped. She didn't want to be this close to him and for one brief second she thought he was going to kiss her. Then she lost her footing on the steps and slid downwards, straight into his waiting arms.

Effortlessly, he lifted her up and started up the steps at a brisk pace with Molly bouncing along beside them, sure this was another fine game to be playing. Kate put her arms around his neck and held on tight, enjoying herself too much to protest.

'What time are you due back at the clinic?' he murmured. He was barely even out of breath.

'My first appointment's at quarter to three,' she said, her heart starting to hammer.

'Good,' he said. 'That means we have plenty of time.'

Kate felt a thrill rush through her body, tingling all the way to her nerve ends. Cory carried her over the threshold before setting her down. His touch was so gentle, so light.

'You all right?' he said.

'Fine,' she replied.

After the warmth outside, the house seemed cool and pleasant, but heat burned in Kate's cheeks.

'I'm so glad you decided to come and work with us, Kate,' he said, but she was hardly listening.

What on earth had she been thinking of to forget herself like that? To allow herself to enjoy the company of a man; to sink into his arms and wallow in the wonder of it all?

She dived across the kitchen and grabbed a ragged scrap of towelling. 'Is this Molly's towel?' she asked.

Molly answered by flinging herself at the towel, growling softly with appreciation as Kate rubbed her soft fur until it stood up in damp spikes. Still Cory remained silent, watching her with a faraway look in his eyes.

Kate returned her attention to the dog, laughing as Molly rolled onto her back, kicking her legs in the air, wriggling from side to side as she rubbed her back on the floor.

'That's enough, Molly,' Cory said, and the dog seemed to sense the tension in his voice. 'Get in your bed now. Good girl.'

With a shake that sent sand spattering around the kitchen, Molly trudged off to her bed and flopped down with a heavy sigh, her pretty brown eyes going from Kate to Cory. Her tail was still wagging, twitching up and down.

Kate folded the towel and put it down and forced herself to meet Cory's gaze. 'Your clothes,' he said. 'Look at the state you're in.'

'It doesn't matter,' she said. 'I can pop home and change before afternoon surgery. Can I help with the lunch?'

She found the way he was looking at her disconcerting to say the least. Then suddenly he seemed to give himself a shake and pull himself up as he answered briskly, 'No, you're all right, I can manage. If you want to wash your hands, there's a bathroom off my bedroom — unless you'd rather go downstairs and use the main bathroom.' He answered her puzzled look with a small smile. 'Living rooms, kitchen and master bedroom on this floor,' he explained. 'Downstairs there are two further bedrooms, the utility room and the bathroom. I use one of the downstairs rooms as a study.'

It was incredible to think, as they surveyed each other across the vast kitchen, that a few minutes ago she had been in his arms. 'I'll, um, I'll go and wash my hands then,' Kate said.

'Through the hall,' he said. 'You can't miss it.'

Kate entered his bedroom and was struck at once by the vastness of it. The midnight-blue carpet felt soft and warm beneath her feet as she stopped for a moment to take stock.

It was a masculine room, sparsely furnished, with big picture windows giving a wonderful view of the sea. There was no clutter, no clothes left lying around, except for a white towelling robe draped over the king-sized bed. She lingered for a while, knowing she shouldn't, but unable to help herself. She was more interested in Cory than she ought to be.

She glanced at the dressing table with various toiletries set out in a neat row beside a hairbrush and comb. And there, in an ornate silver frame, was a photograph of Barbara Leon. A younger Barbara with a slightly plumper face, but no less beautiful. Kate went over to it and picked it up, examining it closely. Barbara's hair was loose around her shoulders, gleaming. Kate remembered what Barbara had said about her man liking her hair long and shuddered, her hand going to her own shorn locks. Scribbled across the bottom right-hand corner of the photograph, she read the words, 'All my love, always, Barbara.'

'Lose your way?'

She spun round at the sound of Cory's voice and with hands that shook guiltily, she carefully replaced the picture. 'She's very beautiful,' she stammered.

'Yes,' he agreed, his tone strangely wistful. 'Yes, she is very precious to me. The bathroom's in here.' He reached out and pushed open the door as if he resented her intrusion into his bedroom, then added, 'Lunch is ready when you are.'

Kate whispered her thanks and hurried into the bathroom, careful not to touch him as she brushed past. She quickly took off her torn tights and scrubbed the sand from her hands before returning to the kitchen, where Cory had already set out their lunch.

Almost as soon as she sat down, Molly appeared beside her, sitting so close that she was pressing her damp fur against Kate's leg.

'Don't give her anything,' Cory warned. 'She knows she's not to beg.'

But Kate couldn't resist those beautiful bright eyes and when she thought Cory wasn't looking, she slipped Molly a tiny piece of bread.

'Don't you ever do as you're told, Kate?' Cory asked, but there was a gleam in his eyes. 'Now go and lie down, Molly. Obviously I can't trust either of you wily females to behave.'

Molly, looking disgruntled, went

back to her bed and flopped down with another almighty sigh.

When the meal was over, Cory made coffee and carried it out to the veranda. 'Tell me about your father, Kate,' he said. 'How long ago was the accident?'

'Four years,' she replied, her eyes fixed on some distant point way out to sea. 'Four years last May.' She was on solid ground again. They'd come through that odd stage of limbo and were speaking to each other on equal terms. For a while nothing had seemed real, and she was greatly relieved at the sudden arrival of normality.

'And your mother was killed in the accident?'

She nodded, a horrible lump forming in her throat. Not only had her father lost his beloved wife, but she had lost her darling mother — and oh how she missed her. Until she'd lost her mother she'd had no idea, no idea at all how much it would hurt.

'Did he grieve? Properly, I mean?' Cory went on with his questioning, apparently unaware of her sudden pain.

But he was aware. He'd seen the shaft of pain light her eyes for a moment when he'd asked about her mother, which was why he'd continued his barrage of questions. She needed help, that much was plain, but the first priority was her father. Cory could see that until David Ross's problems were sorted out, he couldn't even begin to help Kate.

Swamped with guilt that she'd been able to forget her father, even for a little while, Kate forced herself to answer Cory's questions.

'When did this new phase of depression begin, or has he been depressed all the time?'

'There was a brief period when he first came out of hospital,' she said slowly. 'He was hopeful — optimistic almost. Then progress was slow. He became frustrated and angry. He seemed to perk up when we moved here, but he's been slipping down again lately.'

'It must be hell,' Cory said roughly.

'It is,' Kate agreed emphatically. 'Trapped in his own body . . . '

'I was referring to your life, Kate,' Cory cut in, but his voice was laced with sympathy. 'You're a young woman with all of life ahead of you, yet you're trapped, as surely as your father.'

Kate clenched her fists. 'It doesn't feel like that,' she said. 'I love him.'

'I know you do,' he said, reaching across to cover her clenched hands with his and giving them a small squeeze of understanding. 'I don't doubt that for a second.'

She should have drawn her hands away, but felt it was a kindly meant gesture. Besides, she found it comforting just to have someone listen, someone who seemed to understand.

'Four years is a long time,' Cory went on. 'We're not going to solve all your father's problems overnight, but we'll make a start on Monday. Does he take anything in the way of anti-depressants?'

She shook her head. 'He did, for a while, but . . . ' Kate drew in a long, shaky breath and began to wonder if this wasn't all completely hopeless.

'Don't give up,' Cory urged her. 'We'll sort something out, I promise you.'

She looked up sharply. 'You haven't even met him. How can you promise me anything?'

'I never make promises I can't keep,' he said. 'We'll take things slowly at first, but we will need his co-operation. The only way we're going to get that is if he doesn't realise we're trying to help him, and that's where you come in.'

'Me?'

'Yes, you. Just pretend you're madly in love with me and I'll do the same. With any luck he'll be so distracted, he won't realise what we're up to.'

A frown darkened her eyes, making them look black. Pretending to be in love with Cory would be easy as far as she was concerned. But would her father, who was still as sharp as ever, see through Cory's act?

'He's no fool,' she said. 'It won't be easy deceiving him.'

'Maybe not.' Cory grinned, a wicked light shining in his eyes. 'But it's sure going to be fun.'

'I don't think fun is the right word,' she said softly.

'It was thoughtless of me,' he said. 'I'm sorry, Kate.'

'No, I'm the one who should apologise,' she said with a rueful smile. 'I know I take things too seriously and I know I've been really horrible at times lately.'

'Don't you think you may be pushing yourself too hard?'

She was startled by Cory's sudden seriousness and the way he was looking at her, his dark grey eyes boring into hers.

'I don't know what you mean,' she said. 'Compared to my last job, this one's more like a holiday.' She stood up, immediately putting a small distance between them. He stood, too, and towered over her, his eyes searching hers. She didn't like the way he'd turned the conversation so cleverly, making her the topic of the conversation. Any hang-ups she had were her business, no one else's — certainly not Cory Lawrence's.

'I'll help you wash up before I go,' she said, moving towards the kitchen as she spoke, desperate to keep up the distance between them.

'Forget the washing up,' he said. 'You're far more important. Stop running away, Kate.'

She stopped in her tracks, unsure what to say or do next.

'Kate.' He reached out and took hold of her hand. 'It'll only take me a moment to load the dishwasher. I'd far rather talk about you.' His voice was so gentle, yet it went like a laser beam to her heart and gave her a jolt like an electric shock.

'There's nothing to talk about,' she replied earnestly. 'I'm perfectly fine.'

'Are you?' He held tight to her hand.

'Oh, Kate, why won't you trust me? I won't hurt you, I promise.'

Now things really were getting out of hand. She tugged her hand free and started towards the door. 'I have to go home and change before my afternoon surgery,' she said stiffly. 'Thanks for lunch, Cory. It was lovely.' Before he could stop her, she was out of the house and hurrying over to her car. He stood in the open doorway, watching as she jumped in.

If only she'd open up and let him help her, he knew given half a chance, he could. But every time he got anywhere near, she threw up a wall around herself which, try as he might, he couldn't break through.

He waited until she'd driven out of sight before going back inside and closing the door firmly.

'Well, Molly,' he said gruffly, fondling the dog's soft ears, 'at least she seems to like you.'

7

The afternoon surgery began quietly enough, but at four o'clock Kate was called to help out in casualty.

'Sorry,' Gaynor said apologetically. 'Barbara said it was urgent, but she didn't say what the problem was.'

'Never mind, I'll find out soon enough,' Kate said.

As soon as she went through the doors into the hospital, she had a pretty good idea of what was happening. Instead of the usual quiet bustle, all Kate could hear was the sound of rowdy raised voices. They didn't sound angry. Far from it.

Drunks — at four o'clock in the afternoon?

'Thank goodness you're here,' Barbara said, coming to meet her halfway down the corridor. 'The sooner we can sort this lot out and send them on their drunken way, the better.'

'What happened?' Kate hesitated, unwilling to go the last few steps into the casualty department. Her heart was hammering and she felt ridiculously scared. This was broad daylight in a busy little hospital, and although she told herself there was nothing to fear, her mouth was dry from an awful sense of foreboding.

'From what I can gather, this lot were celebrating and got into a fight with some local lads. There don't appear to be any serious injuries, but when they're as far gone as this lot, who can tell? There's a definite broken nose and at least two of them will need stitches.'

Kate pulled herself up and walked into the small reception area. 'Will you be quiet!' she shouted above the racket.

There was a stunned silence and they all turned to look at her in disbelief. Even Barbara was looking surprised.

I've surprised myself, Kate thought proudly. This was the kind of rowdy element the people of the town preferred to discourage, keeping their small tourist haven for families and pensioners, and Kate could see why. 'Thank you,' she said. 'Please sit down and try to behave like reasonable human beings. Nurse Leon and I will deal with you one at a time.' They began to babble and she raised her voice a notch. 'Please remember that this is a hospital. If you can't behave yourselves, I'll have you removed. Is that clear?' She was shaking like a leaf as she took a clipboard from Barbara and scanned the list. 'I'll see Thomas Brownlow first.'

The boy with the broken nose got to his feet and staggered towards her. She led the way into the treatment room. 'In here,' Kate said, drawing back a curtain and pointing the way into a cubicle.

He stumbled in and slumped on the bed. 'I think I'm going to be sick,' he groaned and as if from nowhere, Barbara produced a dish and Kate smiled her thanks.

'Are you all right?' Barbara whispered

before going to treat another casualty.

'I'm fine,' Kate said brightly.

Barbara's beautiful eyes narrowed as she frowned. 'Just remember I'm in the next cubicle if you need me,' she said.

One by one, Kate dealt with the casualties. Most had only superficial wounds which could be easily sorted out with a dab of antiseptic and a light dressing. As they were dealt with, Kate and Barbara sent them on their way until only one remained. He was a tall, slim youth with greasy black hair and an impudent grin. There was nothing friendly about him though. While the other youths had been simply drunk, this one had a different manner. Kate tried not to let her nervousness show as she took him into a cubicle.

'Sit down,' she said. 'What's your problem?' There was nothing obvious. No cuts or bruises.

'I don't like to be kept waiting,' he said.

'I think you should leave and stop wasting my time,' she said and cursed the wobble in her voice.

'I'm not going out there,' he said. 'The police are waiting. I'll stay right here until they've gone.'

He's just a boy, she told herself, *full of his own self-importance.* But he towered over her and she found him intimidating, so she dared not disagree. She couldn't help remembering the night she was mugged and her head began to spin. She'd never forget her fear that night, yet she'd hung on doggedly to her bag, and look where it had got her — in hospital herself! She closed her eyes and swayed, feeling the strength seeping out of her. She wanted to call for help, but no sound would come.

'Leave me alone,' she pleaded.

He picked up on her fear. It obviously made him feel powerful and she felt almost as alone now as she had on that awful night.

'I heard you had a bit of trouble,' Cory said as he strode into the hospital where Barbara was busily cleaning up in the waiting area.

'Ah, the cavalry.' She smiled. 'Too late, Cory. Kate's dealing with the last one now.'

'I saw Sergeant Fox waiting outside mopping them up as they emerge,' Cory said. 'I think he plans to see them away from here as soon as possible.'

'I had Gaynor call him,' Barbara agreed. 'Those lads are trouble, and I don't just mean normal youthful high spirits.' She turned and hurried into the treatment room where only one cubicle had its curtain closed.

Cory followed. 'How did she cope?' he began, then frowned.

'Something wrong, Cory?'

'I don't know. How long have they been in there?'

Barbara caught her breath. 'Ages. Why, Cory? You don't think . . . ?'

Afterwards, he couldn't have said what alerted him that something was wrong; just where Kate was concerned, he seemed to possess some kind of sixth sense. It was a legacy of his days overseas, when there were times when he had had to work on instinct alone.

He moved quickly but silently across to the cubicles. Outside, he thought he heard a strange little noise — the kind a frightened animal might make. Barbara was at his side, an anxious frown on her face.

He ripped the curtain across. The scene that met his eyes made anger bubble up inside him and boil over. There was Kate — tiny, helpless and vulnerable — with a lanky great kid looming menacingly over her. Nothing was happening, but the fear in her eyes stirred him into action. Rage gave him the strength he needed to bodily lift the youth off his feet and carry him kicking and protesting to the hospital entrance, where he flung him outside.

'This one causing trouble was he, Dr Lawrence?' Sergeant Fox asked as he stepped forward, his notebook open and ready. 'I was waiting for him to come out so I could have a few words.

Thought you could hide in the hospital, did you, son?'

The youth dragged the back of his hand across his mouth and glared at Cory with wild, angry eyes.

'He's mad,' he spluttered. 'He tried to kill me.'

'Believe me,' Cory said, his voice low, 'if I'd wanted to kill you, I would have done.' And with that, he spun on his heel and stalked back into the hospital.

When he saw Kate sitting on a chair, white-faced and shaking, all he wanted to do was gather her up in his arms and hold her until her fear subsided. Barbara was crouched down beside her, one arm resting comfortingly around her shoulders.

'Did he hurt you?' he demanded, his voice still rough with anger.

She shook her head. 'No, I'm all right.'

'Of course you're not all right.' His voice was blistering and made Kate wince. 'How can you be? Why on earth didn't you call for help?'

Barbara hugged Kate a little tighter and gave Cory a reproving look. 'Don't you think Kate is upset enough without you pacing up and down and raging like an angry bull? Why don't you do something useful? Go and talk to Sergeant Fox or something.'

His startled look made Kate smile, despite everything. He took one last look at her, then turned around and stomped out.

'Now then,' Barbara murmured. 'I'm going to get you a cup of tea and you and I are going to have a chat.'

'My patients . . . ' Kate began.

'Don't worry. Everything is being taken care of.' She returned within minutes and placed a cup in Kate's hand. 'It's hot and sweet, so drink up.'

Kate sipped the sweet liquid and it ran down her throat, warm and soothing.

'Better?' Barbara asked, and Kate nodded.

'Thanks, Barbara. I feel such a fool. It all seems so silly now.'

'You were terrified out of your wits,' Barbara said. 'If it had been me, I'd have kicked him where it hurts.'

Kate laughed, quite sure that Barbara would have had no compunction about doing just that.

'So why didn't you, Kate? Why didn't you kick him, or yell for help?'

Kate's head dropped and sudden tears burned at her eyes. 'I was mugged,' she said at last, without looking up. 'It was evening, teatime, just starting to get dark. I'd been called out . . . ' She broke off for a moment, calling on all her resources to keep her voice from breaking. 'I knew someone was following me as I went into the lift. As I got in, three men — boys — jumped in behind me. They were wearing masks and one of them had a knife. They only wanted what was in my bag, but like a fool, I hung on to it.'

'Oh, Kate,' Barbara whispered. 'It must have been terrifying.'

'I thought I was going to die, Barbara, and I thought — ' She gave a brittle little laugh. ' — I thought if I'm killed, who will look after my dad?'

Barbara squeezed her shoulder and looked up to see that Cory had come in and had heard everything Kate had said.

'I had a fractured cheekbone and a dislocated jaw and looked as if I'd gone six rounds in a boxing ring when I finally came round. If I'm honest, I suppose I've never really got over it. Before the mugging I wasn't afraid of anything, but now I feel vulnerable and insecure.'

'That's perfectly understandable,' Barbara said. 'But you don't have to cope with all that on your own. Why don't you talk to Cory? He's great with stress.'

Kate laughed off the suggestion and shook off Barbara's concern. 'What have I to be stressed about?' she said lightly. 'Nothing happened. Thanks for the tea, Barbara. Now I really should be getting back to my surgery.'

As she got to her feet, Cory quickly

ducked back out of the door before she could see him. When — if — she ever decided to talk to him, it had to be when she was ready and not before.

★   ★   ★

Monday came round too quickly for Kate. Her father was up early and sitting in the kitchen, discussing the arrangements for the evening with Bea, when Kate came in for her breakfast. She couldn't remember him showing such an interest in anything since before the accident and her heart swelled with love for him, particularly since she knew he was doing it all for her benefit.

'Well, Kate,' he said jovially. 'Tonight I finally get to meet this young man of yours.'

'He's not . . . ' she began, then corrected herself. 'He's not exactly young.'

'You know what I mean.' David waved his hand at her.

'Don't tease the girl,' Bea admonished. 'Can't you see you're embarrassing her?'

He reached out his hand and clasped Kate's. 'I'm sorry, my darling child,' he said. 'I shouldn't tease. It's just that I feel so excited for you.'

She bent down and gave him a giant hug. He was so soft and warm and he smelled so comfortingly familiar. In the days before the accident she would have rushed home to tell him about the incident at the hospital, but now she had to deal with such things on her own. She suddenly felt like weeping. 'Love you, Pa,' she said and turning quickly, grabbed her bag and hurried out before he could see the shine of tears in her eyes.

At the health centre she hurried down the corridor towards her office and walked straight into Cory. His arms came out automatically, his hands resting on her arms to steady her. 'Whoa. Steady on, Kate. You're always in a hurry.'

She looked up into his eyes and her heart lurched. This was the first time she'd seen him since last Friday at the hospital, and she nervously awaited whatever he had to say.

In the event, he didn't mention what had happened but simply asked, 'All set for tonight?'

She brightened. 'Pa's looking forward to it so much. I can't believe the change that's come over him.'

'I'm looking forward to it too,' he said with a heart-stopping grin.

She remembered only too well how it had felt to be held in his arms — how safe she'd felt; how warm and protected . . . and loved? No, not love, of course not love. How could Cory love her when he was already in love with Barbara? She was being silly again, drifting off into the realms of fantasy.

'I should get on,' she said. 'I've a very full schedule today.'

'Me too,' he said ruefully. 'Later, Kate.' And his eyes held a promise that made her heart sing and ache at the same time.

During the busy day, Kate had to find time to see Sergeant Fox and make a statement. It unsettled her a little, having to re-live that frightening experience, but once she immersed herself in her work she found it quite easy to push it to the back of her mind.

Besides, she had something more pressing to worry about. This evening. Cory on her home ground. And it alarmed her to realise she wasn't just worried that her father might cotton on to their ploy. She wanted this evening to be a success for other reasons.

She arrived home to find her father in amazingly high spirits. He'd discarded his usual old trousers and casual shirt for some smart grey slacks and a crisp white shirt.

'You look terrific, Pa,' she said, stooping to drop a kiss on his forehead.

'I've asked Bea to stay and eat with us,' he whispered conspiratorially. 'I hope you don't mind, but she's worked so hard this afternoon. Anyway, I think the poor old girl gets lonely, and it will make up the numbers.'

'I heard that,' Bea snorted as she breezed in from the kitchen. She looked more than offended, she looked mortally wounded; but Kate could see from the glint of humour in her eyes that it was all a pretence. 'And less of the old. Making up the numbers indeed. I've agreed to stay simply to make sure your father behaves himself.'

Kate looked from one to the other. Not for the first time, she suspected that there was a lot of affection between David and Bea. As if all this teasing and banter were there simply to hide something far more meaningful. Or perhaps she was just indulging in a little wishful thinking.

'I'll set the table,' she volunteered. 'Is there anything else I can do, Bea?'

'It's all done,' Bea said.

Kate took extra trouble setting the table, made decorative fans of the white linen napkins and put out a pair of silver candlesticks and a small silver bowl with a few marigolds fresh from the garden. When she'd finished, she stepped back to admire her handiwork.

'It looks lovely,' Bea said. 'He's bound to be impressed.'

Kate flushed. 'I'll have a quick shower and get changed,' she said and dashed off to her room.

It was a warm, humid evening with hardly a breath of air to disturb the curtains. Such a contrast to the brisk, chilly winds of the past few days. But the peninsula was a place of contrasts — and not just where the weather was concerned.

The last thing Kate wanted was to appear hot and flustered, so she chose a feminine silk dress which skimmed her figure, clinging in all the right places. She put on a little make-up and a dab of perfume, and brushed her hair until it shone like a polished conker. For her father's benefit, she told herself firmly.

Her heart fluttered when she looked out and saw Cory's car pull up outside.

'He's here!' she cried, sounding more like a teenager waiting for a first date than a grown woman.

She heard her father's low chuckle as she dashed off to open the door. Cory stood on the threshold, devastatingly handsome in a cream shirt and black trousers, his jacket slung casually over one shoulder. He looked her up and down, his eyes twinkling wickedly. In his hands he held a beautiful bouquet of red roses.

'You look gorgeous, Kate,' he said. 'Really lovely.' There was something so inviting and tantalising about her soft skin. And was he imagining it, or was there very real pleasure in her eyes?

'Flowers, for me? Oh, thank you,' she said, burying her face in the blooms and inhaling the scent. 'I can't remember the last time anyone gave me flowers. Come in,' she urged breathlessly. Taking his hand, she led him through to the living room. 'Pa, Bea, this is Cory Lawrence.'

The meal was a surprisingly relaxed

affair. Once or twice, Kate cast an anxious glance in her father's direction. He looked a little tired, but was determined to give his best and he was doing it for her. A few times he lost concentration, but Cory was patient and there were no awkward moments or excruciating silences.

David was absolutely charming and Kate was over the moon to see something of the man she'd thought killed in that accident along with her mother. He was still there. Deep down inside, her beloved Pa still existed. It made her heart jump for joy.

Throughout the meal, Cory and Kate shared little intimacies. He'd take her hand and press it to his lips, and their eyes would meet and linger as if they were real life lovers. David noticed, as he was meant to, and looked delighted.

It was so easy to pretend to be in love with him. So easy that Kate almost felt it could be real. She could so easily love this man. Every time his lips brushed her hand, she felt thrills race to her nerve endings. Only once did he stoop to kiss her on the lips. It was a brief kiss, but Kate's lips were tingling all evening.

The meal over, Bea insisted that the washing-up should be left as they went to sit in the comfortable lounge area. Cory sat down on the sofa and held out his hand to Kate, pulling her down beside him and casually draping his arm around her shoulders. Kate snuggled up to him, glorying in the feeling of belonging. *Don't forget it's just pretend,* she reminded herself time and time again. *It's not real. We're actors on a stage playing our parts to perfection.*

'Kate tells me she's holding a well-woman clinic,' David remarked, and Kate supposed it was inevitable the conversation should eventually turn to shop talk. 'Splendid idea. My old practice had one which proved extremely successful.'

'I'm sure ours will be, too,' Cory

said, removing his arm from around Kate and sitting forward. 'The emphasis now has shifted from treatment to prevention, don't you agree?'

'Certainly,' David said. 'Educating people to eat well and eat wisely; to take some responsibility for their own well-being.'

Kate closed her eyes. She felt exhausted, tired out by her own fears and anxieties. She needn't have worried, though, as everything had gone absolutely perfectly. And now her father was doing the unthinkable: he was talking about his work, which was something he hadn't done since before the accident. She woke up some time later to find it was beginning to get dark outside and her father and Cory were still engaged in conversation, talking now about the great strides made in transplant surgery.

Bea caught Kate's eye and stifled a yawn. 'They've been talking shop all evening,' she said. 'If I hear any more, I think I'll probably faint. So if you don't mind I'll say good night.'

Kate fetched Bea's jacket and went with her to the door. 'Thank you for this evening,' Kate said, kissing the older woman's cheek.

'Oh, I enjoyed myself.' Bea smiled a little sadly. 'Your father's right when he says I'm a lonely old woman. I am.'

'Not so much of the old,' Kate reminded her. 'I mean it, Bea — thank you from the bottom of my heart. I noticed how everything on the table was cut up small so that Pa could manage without any trouble.' Bea flushed a little and demurred, then hurried off to her car.

When Kate returned to the living room, she noticed that her father was looking tired. 'I'd like to go to bed now, Kate,' he said wearily, with an apologetic look in Cory's direction. For the first time all evening, he looked uncomfortable. As always, he now had to face the indignity of not being able to put himself to bed.

He said good night to Cory and Kate

pushed him through to his bedroom. 'I feel such a helpless old fool,' he muttered as she helped him to undress. 'You should be out there with your young man, not stuck in here seeing to me.'

'Stop it, Pa,' Kate said tiredly. 'Cory understands. You wouldn't think any less of someone because they'd been hurt in an accident which wasn't even their fault, would you?'

'Of course not.'

'Then why should Cory?'

Once he was in bed, he said, 'Aren't you going to ask me?'

'Ask you what?' she said, puzzled.

'Whether or not I like him?'

'I think the answer to that is obvious,' she laughed. 'You do like him, don't you, Pa?'

'Yes.' His reply was unequivocal. He didn't enlarge on it; he didn't have to. The one word was enough. If only it was for real, Kate thought as she kissed him good night.

When she returned to the living

room, Cory was standing outside on the veranda looking out to sea. The moon was sparkling on the water, sending a long, silvery shadow rippling across the surface, and the first few stars were visible in the night sky.

Plucking up her courage, Kate stepped outside and stood beside him. 'I think this evening was a success,' she said.

'In more ways than one,' he agreed. 'It's good to see you relaxing, Kate. You should unwind more often.'

She turned away, but he was too quick for her and reaching out, turned her chin so she had to face him. Even in the moonlight, his eyes sparkled dangerously, perhaps more so than usual. She trembled. 'I know about the mugging, Kate,' he said gently. 'I want to help.'

'Barbara had no right to tell you.' She flared as colour flooded into her cheeks.

'You're not over it, love. You can't be,' he went on. 'On its own, I've no doubt you could have coped; but coming on top of everything else, it's too much. It's bad enough losing your mother, but having to nurse your father and then working under extremely stressful conditions . . . '

Kate swung right away from him, her hands grasping the rail that ran around the edge of the deck. How could Barbara betray her like that? She'd spoken to her in confidence, yet she obviously couldn't wait to tell Cory all the awful details.

Stop it, a poignant little voice cried out, begging Kate to stop torturing herself, but she paid no heed. She rounded on Cory, her dark eyes blazing furiously. 'You've done what you came to do. Now I think you'd better leave.'

Cory cursed himself. Why hadn't he waited, and exercised some of the patience he was famous for? Why did he have to go charging in, both barrels blazing, instead of giving her the time she so badly needed? Why — ? Because he cared about her, and he wasn't about to apologise for caring about someone.

'I said you should go, Cory,' she repeated. 'I want you to leave right now.'

He stared at her for a long, long time before finally speaking. 'Very well, if that's what you want.'

No, no it's not what I want. I don't know what I want anymore, a voice inside Kate cried. But she couldn't say the words.

'For the record, Barbara told me nothing. I overheard you talking to her. Barbara would never betray a confidence.' He turned and picked up his jacket, then with a last pained look at her, he hurried off to his car.

She was still standing outside, shivering in the sudden chill of the night as his car drew away.

8

'I wouldn't be at all surprised if we didn't have a storm on the way,' Bea said the following morning. 'They say we get two days of hot weather, then a thunderstorm, and it's been getting muggier and muggier.'

'Old wives' tale,' David scoffed. 'You'll be telling us you dangle seaweed out of the window to predict the weather next.'

'You wait and see,' Bea said huffily. 'I can feel a storm brewing. My head feels thick and my legs ache. A sure sign.'

Kate was distracted and not really paying attention. She'd enough to think about with the storms in her own life without worrying too much about the real thing.

'I'll take in those hanging baskets and batten down anything that needs it when it happens,' Bea said.

'If,' David corrected. 'If it happens.'

'In fact I'll do it now,' Bea went on. 'Better safe than sorry.' With that, she hurried outside and began to take the hanging baskets down from their brackets.

'You seem very chirpy this morning, Pa,' Kate remarked. 'Did you sleep well?'

'Like a log,' he said. 'When will Cory be coming round again?' He looked like a child, so eager, with his eyes all full of hope.

'Oh, I don't know,' Kate said vaguely, and she could hardly bear to see the disappointment in his eyes. He really did enjoy last night.

'He seems to be very fond of you,' he remarked, his innocent observation sending a knife through her heart. 'He spoke very highly of you.'

'Oh, I think Cory's just a warm, open human being,' she said, and realised that she really believed that.

'Don't frighten him away — not for my sake, Kate,' he said suddenly. 'If you only knew how it made me feel last night, seeing you behaving like a young woman your age should, instead of a . . . ' He broke off and looked so haggard and sad that her heart ached for him.

'I've never done anything for you that I didn't want to, Pa,' she insisted. 'I love you.' And before she knew what she was doing, she was promising, 'Of course I'll ask Cory round again. I just didn't want to over-tire you, that's all.'

He perked up. 'Good girl.'

'There, that's the baskets done,' Bea said, coming in and slapping her hands together. 'Better let Kate get off to work, or she'll be late. Now, what do you want for your breakfast this morning, Doctor?'

'Well, I don't know what I want,' he said contrarily. 'I haven't had a chance to think yet.'

'If you're going to be awkward about it, you'll have cornflakes and like it,' Bea huffed with a playful wink at Kate, who managed a smile in return. Kissing her father goodbye, she set off for work knowing she'd have to keep up this pretence with Cory, but knowing too that it was going to be terribly difficult.

Wednesday dawned gusty and squally and Bea was delighted that her predictions had come true, especially since David had teased her mercilessly about taking the hanging baskets in.

'Have you asked Cory round yet?' David asked Kate as she prepared to leave the house.

'Not yet, Pa,' she said evasively. 'I'll get round to it. I didn't see him yesterday because he was at the District General doing his stint in theatre.'

'Don't leave it too long,' he said.

'I won't. And I won't be home for lunch today as it's my first well-woman clinic. I'm going to have lunch with Barbara and we're going to discuss our plan of action.'

'You make it sound like a military operation,' Bea commented.

'Ah, they've got to be in tune with

each other,' David put in knowledgeably. 'That's half the battle, having a good doctor-nurse relationship. I had a marvellous nurse. Do you remember her, Kate?'

'Jenny,' Kate recalled. 'Yes, I remember.'

'Patients used to mistake her for my wife.' He chuckled wickedly. 'We were that close.'

'Didn't your wife mind?' Bea asked incredulously.

'Of course not. She was a nurse herself and understood the relationship. Anyway, I don't think I could have worked with someone I was having an affair with. The last thing my mind would have been on was the job.'

Kate smiled. She knew that wasn't true. Just look at the way Cory and Barbara worked together. The smile faded and was replaced with a frown. She excused herself abruptly and left for work.

Lunch was a salad roll in the Wyatt's Cove Café on the promenade, and the two women talked about everything but work. Kate liked Barbara. They had got off to a shaky start, but now, it seemed, they were firm friends.

It was fun to talk about ordinary things — about the new blind Barbara had bought for her bathroom which had nearly caused a riot in her house when one of her cats got his claw caught in the string-pull. About silly things that happened every day which weren't at all extraordinary, but which made up the fabric of life. Kate couldn't remember the last time she'd had a conversation to match this. It was just so wonderfully relaxing.

Barbara also talked about her various jobs around the world. Not only was she beautiful, but she was interesting as well. This change in her attitude, Kate realised, was a step forward in itself. She'd gone a little way to stopping suspecting everyone's motives, to accepting that people were ready and willing to help her.

When it was time to leave, Barbara

stepped outside and had her breath snatched away by the wind. 'What a day,' she said. 'Still, perhaps a good storm is what we need to blow this awful oppressive heat away.'

'Let's hope so,' Kate agreed. 'It makes everyone short-tempered.'

Arms linked like lifelong friends, Kate and Barbara ran the short distance to the health centre and arrived giggling like schoolgirls. Kate hurried down to her surgery and Barbara joined her a few minutes later.

'What have we got this afternoon?' Barbara asked when she saw the list on Kate's desk. 'Are those all appointments?'

'They are.' Kate grinned. 'And I've told Gaynor to squeeze anyone in that comes through the door. The last thing I want to do if someone has plucked up courage to come here is frighten them off.'

Barbara was silent and when Kate looked up, it was to find the nurse staring at her.

'What is it?'

'I was just thinking,' Barbara said. 'I can see why Cory was so keen to take you on. You're very like him, you know.'

'I am?'

'Oh, yes. Don't be fooled by appearances. There was a time when he was just as aloof as you try to be.'

Kate had no time to ask what she meant, for at that moment Gaynor buzzed through to say the first patient was on her way.

'That will be our first customer,' Kate said. 'Anne Harris. I have her blood test results. She's likely to be rather nervous, so . . . '

'You don't have to tell me.' Barbara smiled as there was a tentative little knock on the door. She stood up, opened the door and gave Anne a brilliant welcoming smile. 'Come through to the examination room,' she said. 'Dr Ross will be with you in a moment.'

When the examination was over, Anne breathed a sigh of relief. 'You don't know how nervous I was about coming here today,' she admitted.

'Yes, I do,' Kate said with a smile. 'And you should be very pleased with yourself, Anne. Did your husband come with you?'

She rolled her eyes. 'He's in the waiting room. He didn't trust me to come on my own.'

'It's nice that he cares,' Kate said warmly. 'Some men wouldn't bother.'

'I know,' Anne sighed. 'So what do you think?'

'Well, the tests confirm that you are anaemic. I can give you something for that. You should feel better in no time. Everything else looks fine. Barbara will give you a diet sheet which will also help boost your energy and ensure the iron is properly absorbed.

'Thank you so much,' Anne said. 'I feel better already just knowing something can be done.'

At the end of a very long afternoon, Barbara sat down with a sigh and kicked off her shoes, curling her toes.

'What a crowd,' she said. 'You'd think we were giving away free balloons or something. I must say, Cory was right about this one.'

'Was there any doubt?'

'I thought he was being silly, wanting a woman to do the well-woman clinic — sexist, you know? I even accused him of shoving work he didn't particularly like onto someone else. But I think it's paid off. I suppose I shall have to apologise and eat humble pie.'

'Is that what you meant before about me being the token woman?' Kate asked candidly.

Barbara smiled. 'Did I say that? Oh I'm sorry, Kate. What a rotten thing to say. I suppose deep down I was feeling jealous. I've been the number-one woman in Cory's life for so long now, I suppose I felt threatened by the arrival of another woman. Silly really.' She broke off and gave a little laugh.

Well at least I know where I stand, Kate thought. 'You've no need to worry on that score,' she said firmly. 'I've no designs on Cory Lawrence.'

Barbara jumped up suddenly. 'Lord, is that the time? I'm supposed to be collecting my wedding invitations and hymn sheets from the printers today.' Kate was knocked for six. This was the first she'd heard of a wedding. Not that she kept abreast of the gossip. It was one of the many disadvantages of keeping yourself to yourself. So Barbara and Cory were to be married.

'You're getting married,' she whispered, the news shocking her more than she'd ever care to admit.

'Whoops.' Barbara put her hand to her mouth. 'Do me a favour, Kate, and keep it under your hat for the time being. We don't want it getting out as public knowledge just yet, though I suppose everyone in Wyatt's Cove must realise it's on the cards. That's the trouble in a job like ours. You become public property.'

'I won't say anything,' Kate managed to mumble.

'Thanks. Just make like you're

surprised when you get your invitation. There's a certain pecking order around here when it comes to news and if Gaynor isn't first with it, then there's hell to pay.' With that, Barbara dashed off, leaving Kate to tidy up the loose ends.

'How did the clinic go?' Cory asked, poking his head round the door. Her heart started to go faster just at the sight of him, but she managed to keep her cool. Perhaps she should congratulate him, but on second thought, Barbara said she wanted it kept quiet. She didn't want to drop Barbara in it.

'Busy,' she admitted. 'We had several women come in on the off-chance without an appointment. I made a point of asking if it made a difference me being a woman doctor, and I have to say that several women said it did.'

'Hm, I thought so,' he said, rubbing his chin thoughtfully. Kate listened to his fingers rasping on his bristles and caught his eye. He grinned. 'I know! I could use a shave.'

'I'm not saying anything.' Kate put up her hands in a defensive gesture. 'If you like the unkempt look, it's up to you.'

'To think, when I was a lad I used to shave three times a day to try to encourage growth. Now if I don't shave, I end up looking like a yeti by teatime. I'm glad the afternoon went well. You got along well with Barbara, I assume? She's an excellent nurse.'

'Yes,' Kate agreed. 'She is.' A terrific gust of wind blew against the window, driving rain into the glass and making Kate jump.

'Better batten down the hatches,' Cory said. 'It's going to get worse tonight. They were putting out a severe weather warning on the radio earlier.'

'It's already done.' She smiled. 'Bea's sixth sense was quicker than the Met Office.'

He turned to leave, then stopped in the doorway and turned back to face her. 'By the way, your father called this afternoon.'

'My father?' She gave a start, but his smile reassured her that there was nothing to worry about.

'He's invited me over on Sunday.'

'Lunch?'

'The whole day.'

'You didn't accept of course,' she said.

'I most certainly did.' He grinned.

'He never mentioned it to me,' she said. 'He's been asking when you'd be coming over again, but I never thought he'd ring you himself.'

'Oh, he didn't ring me, Kate,' Cory said. 'He called in with Bea.' He broke off and considered for a moment. 'Don't tell him I told you. He probably wants to surprise you.'

'He's done that all right,' she said, delighted. 'I can't believe that he came all the way here. It's wonderful news, Cory.'

'Yes, isn't it,' he said.

'Cory, wouldn't you prefer to spend Sunday with Barbara?'

He looked puzzled, a frown sending

131

deep lines running across his forehead. 'Barbara's got a lot on this weekend,' he replied.

As Kate drove home through the storm, she could feel the wind buffeting the car on the exposed roads. Rain lashed the windscreen and ran in streams along the gutters.

She was still reeling from the news that her father had been to the health centre. Since they'd moved to Wyatt's Cove he hadn't left the house at all, not even to go as far as the shops.

She pulled up outside the bungalow and stepped out into the driving rain. Far below, the sea was crashing against the rocks and she could taste the salt spray on her lips. Just as well Bea had taken in the hanging baskets, she thought, otherwise the poor plants would have been smashed to pieces.

As she walked in, Bea was already putting on her raincoat. 'I'm afraid a fence panel has come down. I'll get Phil Scott to come up and put it back for you when the storm has gone. I'm getting off early so I can check if there's any damage to my cottage, though I don't expect there to be as it's fairly sheltered where I am. I've left a couple of pasties in the oven for your dinner.' She opened the door and looked out, wrinkling her nose. 'Look at that sky.'

'How has he been today?' Kate asked.

'He was full of himself this morning, but his enthusiasm began to flag around lunchtime. He got cross and crotchety, but he had a nap and woke up as perky as ever. He really seems to have taken to Dr Lawrence.' She gave Kate a searching look, but Kate wasn't prepared to give anything away.

'Drive home carefully,' she said.

'I will,' Bea said and hurried out into the storm.

David was sitting in the lounge facing the rain-lashed windows when Kate walked in. He was listening to music on his MP3 player with his eyes closed, and didn't realise Kate was there until she switched it off.

'What?' His eyes flew open. 'What did you do that for? Oh, Kate, it's you.' His cross look vanished and he looked pleased to see her. 'I've been to see Cory,' he burst out, and he looked so proud she could have hugged him on the spot, but that would have given the game away.

'Been to see him?' she repeated. 'Pa, have you been out of the house?'

'I've been to the health centre. I would have popped in to see you, but the receptionist said you were busy. So what do you think, Kate?'

'Oh, Pa, I'm so pleased.' Now she could hug him. 'But what made you go out? Are you not feeling well?'

'I'm as fit as a fiddle. Just because I'm confined to this contraption doesn't mean there's anything wrong with my general health. No, you've got the wrong idea entirely. I went to see Cory to ask him over for the day on Sunday. Well, you were dragging your heels, so I took the bull by the horns so to speak, and . . . '

She turned away so he wouldn't see that she wasn't happy about him inviting Cory over. The man had a life of his own to lead; he wouldn't want to waste his time coming round here again.

'Time spent on people is never time wasted,' she remembered him saying, and realised that they weren't just empty words. He'd meant them. But was that how he saw her and her father — as good causes? And once their problems were all magically solved, would he move on to his next worthy project?

'I thought he could bring his little dog along,' David went on, oblivious to Kate's discomfort. 'I've heard so much about her, and she sounds a real little character.'

'She's a proper little Herbert.' Kate chuckled.

'And I've asked Bea to come over as well,' he added, a trifle sheepishly.

'You really are a dark horse, aren't you, Pa?' Kate laughed.

'No,' he protested. 'She's been so good, putting up with my sour moods.'

'So you thought you'd make up a nice, cosy little foursome,' Kate teased.

'Certainly not. I'm asking Bea simply to . . .'

'Make up the numbers?' She ruffled his thinning hair. 'Of course you are, Pa.'

Kate couldn't remember the last time she'd spent such an enjoyable evening with her father. He wanted to know all about her first well-woman clinic and she was just as eager to talk about its success. He'd asked about her work before, but this was the first time his interest had seemed genuine. In the past, Kate always had the feeling he was just asking because she expected him to. It wasn't until after she'd helped him to bed that she allowed herself to think of Cory. It was going to break Pa's heart when he found out Cory was going to marry Barbara.

She cleared up quickly and went to

bed. Even the double-glazing couldn't keep out the noise of the storm as it raged all around. Lightning flashed and flickered, lighting up the bungalow from all directions, and Kate lay in bed with her curtains open, watching the storm. She'd heard that they had spectacular storms on the peninsula, where they'd go round and round for hours at a time. She could even hear the crack as forked lightning zig-zagged across the sky.

For a while it seemed that the storm was directly overhead, and the little bungalow seemed to shake with every crash. But then the noise began to abate and she slipped into a childhood habit of counting the seconds between flash and bang. It lulled her to sleep.

She woke with a start to find the world plunged into darkness. There was no light from the street lamps out on the road, no red glow from the digits on her radio alarm. It was still raining, coming down hard and fast, and the wind was gusting around the eaves. Bea, with her weather lore, had said that a gusty wind could do more damage than a good steady blow.

She felt uneasy. *It's just a storm,* she told herself, but her feelings of unease grew with every mysterious creak and bang she heard. She tried to switch on the bedside light, but knew even before it was confirmed for her that the power was off. Was it the whole town or just the bungalow? she wondered.

'Stop worrying,' she told herself out loud. 'It's just a power cut. Nothing to worry about. It'll probably be fixed by morning.'

She buried herself under the covers and jumped again when she heard the dustbin roll down the side of the bungalow, crashing against the wall as it went. At least, she hoped it was just the dustbin.

It was no use. She couldn't get back to sleep no matter how hard she tried.

Perhaps Pa was having difficulty sleeping too, although he was sleeping like the proverbial log lately.

'I can't even make myself a cup of tea,' she grumbled as she climbed out of bed.

Then she heard the crash and the splintering sound of breaking glass. Unable to find her slippers in the darkness, she hurried barefoot through the bungalow and looked out of the kitchen window. The little lean-to conservatory had gone. She blinked and tried to see more, but it was impossible in the darkness.

A knot of fear formed in her stomach. Grabbing a torch, she went through to the living room. The bungalow felt as if it was shaking, if a building could tremble with fear. Pushing aside the sliding door, she stepped out onto the veranda and was soaked to the skin in an instant.

She didn't know what she had been expecting to find, but it wasn't this. Shock rendered her helpless. Part of the veranda had gone, having slipped downwards and away. In the dim beam of her torch she could see rocks and rubble being washed down the cliff towards the beach and the raging, boiling sea beneath.

9

With trembling hands, she picked up the phone, but the line was dead. No power, no phone. Her mobile phone had no signal.

'Oh, Lord,' she whispered. Perhaps she was over-dramatising things when she thought that the bungalow might slip down the cliff at any moment, but the precarious position which had seemed so wonderful when she first saw the place now seemed deadly. And if the bungalow did start to slide, her father lay helpless in his bed.

'Pa!' She rushed through to his bedroom, grabbing her mac as she went and dragging it on over the top of her sodden pyjamas.

He was sound asleep and when she shook him awake, she heard his voice, soft and reassuring. 'It's all right, sweetheart. It's just a storm,' he said sleepily in the same reassuring tones he would have used when she was a child and afraid.

'No, Pa. Wake up. Listen. We've got to get out.'

He came properly awake then and she heard his sharp intake of breath as he heard the storm.

The torch she had placed on his bed was losing power, its light growing dimmer and dimmer until it faded completely. Kate picked it up and shook it, but it was finished.

'Oh, no!' She grabbed his chair, struck her shin in the darkness and bit hard on her lip to stop herself crying out with the sudden sharp pain.

'Where will we go?' he asked, and sounded so unsure of himself and afraid that it wrenched at her heart. He must never have been as acutely aware of his vulnerability as he was right now, nor more conscious of his total and complete helplessness.

'I don't know,' she answered as she fumbled in the pitch-blackness to get him seated safely in his chair. Dragging a blanket from the bed, she wrapped it tightly around his legs, then she began to push.

Obstacles seemed to stop her at every turn. Her home became a strange place full of objects she didn't even know existed.

'Slow down,' David said calmly, his voice steady and sane in the madness of the storm. 'Take a deep breath, Kate, and move slowly. We'll get out if we take things nice and easy.'

His voice penetrated the fog of terror in her mind and she stopped for a moment, drawing in deep breaths until she felt steady enough to move forward again. Yes, she was afraid, but she'd been in worse situations than this and she knew everything depended upon her keeping a cool head.

'We're coming up to the doorway. Slow down and I'll feel our way. A little to the left, Kate. That's it, darling.'

They progressed painfully slowly, with him feeling the way ahead and calling out directions for Kate to follow. They were out in the hall when there was a sudden gut-wrenching lurch and the floor seemed to disappear from under her feet. 'It's like being on a boat on rough seas, Kate. It feels worse than it is.' His voice was calm and reassuring.

She took a deep breath and moved forward, only to have the chair suddenly wrenched downwards. It took all her strength to pull it back and she sobbed with the effort.

'It's all right now, Kate,' David said firmly. 'I think the floor has probably collapsed. We'll have to find another way out.' He sounded so calm, as if he was talking about a milk bottle blowing over in the wind.

She wrestled the chair away from the hole and cried out when there was an almighty crash. Windows smashed and the rain and wind came in, relentless and chilling.

'Damn this chair!' David raged, his former calm now leaving him. 'Leave me here, Kate. Get yourself out.'

It brought her to her senses. 'I'm doing no such thing,' she said stubbornly. 'I leave this bungalow with you or not at all.' She heard his low chuckle in the darkness below the fury of the storm and couldn't help smiling, despite their terrible predicament.

But try as she might, she still couldn't find a safe route out. She'd taken to pulling the chair rather than pushing it, using her foot to feel ahead for the points where the floor had collapsed. There was no gaping hole, but it was a trap for the wheelchair and she had no intention of letting her father get stuck in a hole. Her feet stung as she trod on slivers of broken glass, but she was almost oblivious to pain, as if her body had taken control, focusing everything on the will to escape.

It's hopeless, she thought. She'd completely lost her bearings now and might just as well have been in a strange house for all the sense anything made to her.

Suddenly she felt a hand on her arm and the wheelchair was pulled out of her grasp. 'You won't get out that way,' Cory's voice said, and she felt weak with relief. 'We'll have to double back and try to get out through the kitchen.'

'Cory!'

'Hold on to me,' he said. 'Come on, Kate, this is no time to be coy. Grab my jacket and hang on.'

She did as she was told, following right up behind him as he manoeuvred the wheelchair through the wreckage of the bungalow. In no time, it seemed, after the eternity she had been struggling alone, they were outside. Kate saw a blue flashing light and suddenly a fireman had his arms around her and was steering her away from the bungalow, following Cory as he hurried ahead, pushing her father towards his car.

In a moment of pure selfishness, she wished it were Cory's arms that were wrapped around her, holding her safe. It was only a brief thought, but it made her more determined than ever to keep him at arm's length.

★   ★   ★

The full force of what had happened didn't hit Kate until she was sitting in Cory's warm, bright kitchen. The power had come back on just after they had arrived. Molly was sitting beside her, her head and one paw resting in Kate's lap as she gazed adoringly up at her.

She felt devastated, totally destroyed. There were no words to describe how utterly and completely lost she felt.

Her home — the fresh start she'd planned for herself and her father — lay in ruins. Yet to look at him, you'd think nothing awful had happened. He was drinking cocoa and talking animatedly to Cory, while Cory tended to his minor injuries.

'She might only be little, but she's incredibly strong,' David said. 'Even as a child, she was always a gutsy little thing. I think even if you hadn't turned up when you did, she'd have got us out of there somehow.'

'I've no doubt,' Cory said and he looked across to where Kate was sitting, her huge eyes looking totally empty as she gazed sightlessly into space. She looked small and helpless and in desperate need of a hug, but Cory was busy tending to her father. *Later*, he promised himself. *Later I'll hold her in my arms and try to soothe some of her pain.*

'Do you think we've completely lost the bungalow?' David asked.

'We've lost places like that before in the town,' Cory said. 'But most are pretty well built and often, with a bit of good repair work, they can be put right.'

'Really?' David said. 'You mean it's not going to slide down the cliff?'

'No, I shouldn't think so,' Cory laughed warmly. 'You've lost your conservatory, but the foundations of the bungalow are deep and strong. These things always seem a lot worse in the darkness. It'll probably look a lot better in the light of day.'

'It's just a matter of what we do in the meantime, I suppose,' David said wistfully.

'Well, you'll stay here with me of course,' Cory said at once. 'I've plenty of room.'

Kate looked up then and blinked as she took in what Cory was saying. 'We couldn't possibly . . . ' she began.

'Nonsense, of course we could,' David said firmly. 'Cory wouldn't have offered if it was likely to put him out. It's not so bad, Kate. Didn't you hear what Cory was saying? They'll probably be able to fix our place for us.'

She looked from her father to Cory. They were both smiling at her — David happily, and Cory . . . Cory's smile was different. His was strangely wistful and a little sad.

Her gaze moved to his eyes and she

149

felt something inside her jolt, something which was infinitely more powerful than the unleashed fury of the storm. Quickly, she averted her eyes to look at her father.

She saw his smile begin to waver. Good grief, if he could still smile after all that had happened, then so could she. They were still alive and had lost nothing that couldn't be replaced.

Instead of sitting here feeling sorry for myself, I should be rejoicing, Kate thought. *So why aren't I?*

'There, that's you all patched up, David,' Cory said at last. 'You'll probably have some bruising on your arms, but there's nothing we need worry about. You can have my bed, as the other rooms are downstairs.'

'Ah, bed,' David sighed. 'Would you be terribly offended if I turned in straight away?'

'Of course not.' Cory smiled.

To Kate's further amazement, Cory took charge, pushing David through to the bedroom and helping him into bed.

She felt almost surplus to requirements as the two men chatted easily. David certainly had no qualms, nor did he seem to suffer any embarrassment as Cory helped him. How much of that was down to Cory? He had a knack for putting people at their ease, a knack that had worked wonderfully with David.

It's just this once, she reminded herself. Putting David to bed once was no big deal. It would be different if he had to do it every day for years to come, as Gareth had so cruelly pointed out.

'I can't see myself being nursemaid to your father,' he'd told her unkindly. 'And that's how I'd end up, because I couldn't be married to you and leave you to carry the burden of it all.'

Kate had more pride than to tell him she'd take full responsibility for her father. And she thought more of her father than to have him foisted on a man who considered him a burden.

'You haven't touched your cocoa.

And you're shivering,' Cory said gently when he returned. 'We should have got you out of those wet things first of all. Let's get that coat off.' Before she could argue or protest, he was tugging off her coat to reveal her sodden pyjamas beneath. He let out a small gasp of shock. 'You're soaked through. Oh, love, why didn't you say something? You shouldn't have been sitting there in those wet things.' He slid his arm around her waist and she leaned against him, drawing strength from him. 'Come on downstairs and I'll run you a hot bath.'

'I've nothing to change into,' she said, her teeth chattering.

'I'll find you something, and tomorrow I'll drive over to your bungalow to see if I can rescue anything for you.'

Slowly and gently, he took her downstairs and through to one of the bedrooms. 'You can sleep in here for the duration,' he said. 'It's best if your father has my room. It would be a nightmare trying to get his chair up and

152

down those stairs.'

'I don't like leaving him,' she murmured sleepily. 'If he calls out during the night I won't know.'

'I'll sleep on the sofa, so if he wakes I'll hear him,' Cory assured her. 'After all you've been through, you need a rest. And I'm not just talking about what happened tonight,' he added under his breath.

Kate heard his muttered aside and lowered her eyes.

'Get out of those wet things and put this around you,' he said, handing her a towelling robe warm from the airing cupboard. 'I'll run your bath.'

The water was wonderfully soothing and Kate could have stayed in it for the rest of the night, but she forced herself to get out and get dry, pulling on the white towelling robe. Her feet were sore, but thankfully most of the cuts were superficial and not too deep. Certainly none would need stitching. She opened the bathroom cabinet and found some antiseptic and a packet of plasters, and set about treating the cuts on her feet. Cory would have insisted on doing it otherwise, and she wasn't sure she could cope with him touching her even if it was only her feet, she thought wryly.

She emerged from the bathroom, her hair forming a dark halo around her pale face, just as Cory appeared downstairs with a steaming mug of cocoa. His smile made her pulse quicken.

'He's sleeping like a baby,' he said. 'I've brought you some more cocoa. Feeling warmer?'

She nodded and followed him through to the bedroom.

'I would have done your feet for you,' he murmured, looking at her poor little feet covered in sticking plasters. 'It must have been awkward doing them yourself.'

'Not really.' She smiled readily. 'There's no serious damage, just rather a lot of it.' She felt incredibly relaxed and sat down on the bed, curling her feet up beneath her, sipping the hot cocoa Cory handed to her. The storm was still raging outside, but it had lost its bite and was in the process of dying. In here, she felt safe and warm. 'Cory, I don't know how to thank you,' she began.

'Then don't.'

'How did you know we needed help? How did you know what to do?'

He gave a sigh, then sat down in a battered peacock chair and stretched his long legs. For a long time he didn't say a word and seemed to be lost in thought. Kate had almost forgotten she'd asked him a question by the time he started to speak.

'I can't explain,' he said. 'Gut instinct I guess. The storm woke me and Molly was unusually restless.' He shrugged. 'I just had the feeling you needed me. And I was right, wasn't I, Kate?' She nodded. 'And I knew what to do when I got there because I've been in similar situations before, finding my way round dark, crumbling houses. Barbara and I were part of a rescue team in China after an earthquake. There were a lot of casualties.'

He looked sad and thoughtful and Kate would have reached out and held his hand as he talked if it wasn't for the spectre of Barbara which refused to go away, even for an instant.

'We've been through a lot together, Barbara and I,' he went on. 'We were in a house together, treating a man with crush injuries. His chances weren't great — in fact, they were pretty dismal — but he had a wife and six kids.' He broke off, looking anguished. 'I don't know if it was an aftershock or what, but there was a landslide, and the house we were in was buried. We lost the patient of course.'

'And you and Barbara?' she prompted gently.

'I almost lost her,' he said, his voice as rough as gravel. 'She came within inches of losing her life. It isn't the only hairy moment in our past, by any means,' he added with a wry smile. 'I guess that's why we work so well together as a team now. Having worked under tremendous pressure, it became vital that we should be able to anticipate the needs of each other.'

It explained so much. No wonder they were so deeply attached. Kate felt awful for allowing her petty jealousy to become so huge. They deserved each other, Barbara and Cory, and she had no right at all to wish it were any different.

Tonight had stirred up all kinds of memories for Cory and he seemed determined to share them with Kate. He talked and she listened. 'It's as if an invisible thread connects us,' he finished. 'When we first got back to England, we could hardly bear to be parted from each other. But of course, eventually we did part. Then I came here and when the vacancy came up at the hospital, I got in touch with Barbara and suggested she should apply.'

Outwardly calm and cool, Kate was in turmoil inside. She liked Barbara and she thought a great deal of Cory. She cared for both of them more than she'd care to admit, and probably the only decent thing she could do now would be to bow out gracefully. Start again somewhere else, somewhere different. Losing the bungalow presented her with the perfect excuse. Even her father would understand if she said she wanted to move on.

'Kate?'

She looked up sharply. 'Did you ask me something?'

'How about you? How are you?'

'Fine.' Her voice sounded artificially bright even to her own ears. She couldn't expect it to fool Cory.

'I'm sorry; it was selfish of me to waffle on. You must be exhausted.'

'No.' She put out her hand and touched his arm. 'I don't mind listening to you, Cory.' *Glutton for punishment, that's me.*

'You've done enough listening. Now it's my turn. Tell me about yourself, Kate.'

'There's nothing much to tell that you don't already know,' she said lightly. She could tell him about Gareth — how he'd broken her heart by deserting her at the very moment she really needed someone to lean on. But mightn't that appear as if she were trying for the sympathy vote? Anyway, if she told him anything at all, he might then go on to relay it to Barbara; and as much as she liked Barbara, she didn't want her private life gossiped about.

'You don't have to be afraid of me Kate,' he said. 'I won't hurt you.'

You already have, if you only but knew it, she thought. *Or maybe I'm just hurting myself.* Even if Cory was interested in her, which he clearly wasn't, she wasn't any freer than he was.

'I think I'd like to go to bed now,' she said.

Cory turned back the covers. 'And straight to sleep. That's an order. I'll find something for you to wear in the morning and I'll leave it outside this room on the chair, OK?'

'Thanks, Cory.'

He mumbled good night and turned away. He wished she'd stop thanking him; he couldn't bear it.

He stopped in the doorway and turned back. She nearly blew him away with her smile and he saw yet another side to Kate Ross. First there was the doctor, capable and rational. Next came the dutiful and loyal daughter, but struggling to get out from under that weighty burden was a woman. Sometimes vulnerable, sometimes strong.

She was so different to Barbara. With Barbara, what you saw was what you got. There were no hidden depths to Barbara, and although she was beautiful and he loved her dearly, he couldn't compare her, or his feelings for her, to Kate.

'Good night,' he said huskily. 'Sleep well.'

10

The next morning, Kate stood in front of the mirror and held out her arms. 'I look like a clown.'

'A very pretty clown,' Cory said.

A sweatshirt and jeans, both belonging to Cory, absolutely drowned her. She had huge turn-ups on the jeans, which were tied around her middle with a belt done up on the tightest notch. The sleeves of the sweatshirt dangled over her hands.

Cory sighed like a weary parent and rolled the sleeves back until her hands were free. 'Better?' He stepped back and looked her up and down. She didn't look at all like a clown. She looked like a little girl who'd been raiding a grown-up's wardrobe, tiny and lost.

'You're laughing at me,' she accused.

'I can't help it. You're such a funny,

loveable little thing.'

'I am not a little thing,' she said. 'It's not my fault I've no shoes.'

'Well, I think you look cute,' he said with an infuriating grin. 'Now come and have some breakfast, and then I'll drive you over to the bungalow. We could collect your car and see if we can get in to fetch some clothes for you.'

'My car keys are in the bungalow somewhere,' she groaned.

'No spares?'

'Yes — in the bungalow.'

'Well, that's handy,' he chuckled.

When he saw her, Kate's father burst out laughing. 'You look like a clown.' he said with a hearty guffaw.

'See?' she cried. 'I told you.'

Molly spotted her and couldn't have cared less what she looked like as she flung herself bodily at Kate's legs.

'Down, Molly,' Cory bellowed authoritatively. Molly took no notice whatsoever and continued to leap and bound in circles, letting out excited little yips of welcome. 'I'm sorry,

162

Kate. She's desperate to go out.'

'Take her,' Kate said. 'I'll get breakfast.'

'Sure?'

He didn't need much persuading, and Kate felt he would have agreed to anything just to stop Molly bounding around.

She soon found what she needed in the kitchen and set about cooking a good breakfast for them all. 'I don't know about you, Pa,' she remarked, 'but I'm starving.'

'Are you feeling all right this morning, Kate? Got many bruises?'

She pulled a face. 'I've got a huge one on my shin and one on my knee, but nothing to worry about. How about you?'

'I'm feeling a bit sore,' he said. 'But it's nothing that won't mend.'

'Cory and I are going over to the bungalow after breakfast. I'll see if I can get some things for you.'

'Cory's given me a few things,' he said. 'We're similarly built, although I have to say where I have fat, Cory has muscle.'

'It needn't be like that you know, Pa, if you'd only get down to the pool and do some exercise. Denise Blair isn't just a physiotherapist; she's also a remedial gymnast.'

The usual rebuke didn't come. Instead, he nearly floored her by saying thoughtfully, 'You know, I might just do that.'

Cory returned with a very damp dog just as Kate was dishing up scrambled eggs and bacon. 'It looks wonderful.'

'I wonder if anyone else lost their home last night,' Kate said as she sat down to eat.

There was a short silence, then Cory said, 'You were the only casualties last night. I've already checked. They think there may have been a mini tornado, which explains why your house suffered so much damage.'

When they'd eaten, David insisted on loading the dishwasher while Cory drove Kate over to the bungalow. On her feet she wore a pair of wellington boots which Cory said he kept as spares for visitors, but which looked suspiciously as if they might fit Barbara.

The wind had dropped, but everywhere was still wet. Kate got out of the car and stood still, staring at the wreckage of her home. Her eyes took it all in: the smashed shrubs, the broken windows, the door crudely boarded up where it had been hanging from its hinges. Leaves and twigs littered the garden.

She stumbled suddenly, but Cory was ready to catch her, his strong arms folding around her protectively. She leaned against him as her strength ebbed away. 'Oh, Cory,' she whispered. 'What a mess.'

'It's not as bad as it looks, love.'

A team of men was still working on the bungalow, making it safe and secure. Cory waited until he sensed the initial shock had passed, then he moved forward, holding her close.

'Do you think I'll be able to get any

of my things?' she asked shakily.

'I'll ask. Stay here.' He let her go reluctantly, then strode off to talk to the man in charge. Kate watched and saw a lot of head-shaking going on. A kind of desperation took hold. If she couldn't get her things, how could she go to work? People weren't going to be very impressed with a doctor who looked like a clown.

At last Cory returned. *Has he any idea at all how gorgeous he is?* Kate thought as he flicked his hair aside — or was it just her heart that fluttered at the mere sight of him? *You've got to put a stop to these thoughts right now,* she told herself firmly. *It's going nowhere, and if you had half the sense you were born with, you'd have realised that by now.*

'It's no go, I'm afraid,' Cory said apologetically. 'They want to make sure it's safe before letting you in to fetch any of your clothes. Apparently there's a danger that the whole thing is unstable and could slide down the cliff at any moment. Don't look so worried, love; they have to look at the worst-case scenario. Off the record, they reckon once it's been assessed by the structural engineer, you'll be able to get in with no problems.'

'Oh, right,' Kate whispered. Then she saw a familiar figure labouring up the hill on a bike. 'Here's Bea. My goodness, I should have phoned her to let her know what was happening. She'll be expecting to give Pa his breakfast.'

The cycle's brakes squealed as Bea came to a halt beside Cory's car. Her mouth dropped open, her eyes widened and she cried, 'What on earth happened? Where's David?'

'David is at my house,' Cory told her. 'He wasn't hurt and neither was Kate. How did you fare in the storm?'

'Didn't even hear it and it was so nice this morning, I decided to leave my car at home and come on my bike,' Bea said, without taking her eyes off the bungalow. 'What a mess. Has the conservatory gone? Oh, that'll be all those dear little geranium cuttings gone too.'

Kate and Cory exchanged looks. There was the bungalow on the brink of falling onto the beach, and Bea was lamenting the loss of a few plants. Kate saw the glint in Cory's eyes, and together they laughed out loud. They weren't meaning to mock Bea, or make fun of her, but it just struck them both as so funny.

'It isn't funny,' Bea said huffily. 'Your father and I spent a whole afternoon dipping those cuttings into hormone rooting powder and planting them.' She broke off and Kate was alarmed to see tears shimmering in her eyes. She stopped laughing at once and went to put her arms around the woman who had been their house-keeper and had come to mean so much more.

'Oh, Bea, I'm sorry. We didn't mean to hurt your feelings, did we, Cory?'

'Of course not. It's just us being silly.

This must have come as an awful shock to you, Bea.'

Bea managed a little smile. 'Well, it did, and it is daft to get all upset over a few plants. The most important thing is that no one was hurt. So what happens now? Where will you go?'

'Kate and David will be staying with me until the bungalow can be repaired,' Cory said.

'Or until we can make other arrangements,' Kate added quickly, reminding both herself and Cory that this should be nothing more than a temporary solution. He'd probably be as glad to get rid of Kate and her father as she would be to get away.

Kate noticed that Bea was looking lost and unsure of herself, but before she could say anything to reassure her, Cory said, 'You're welcome to carry on working for Kate and David at my house if you'd like. Although I think you're more than a housekeeper now, aren't you?' Kate was amazed to see the older woman blush. 'David will still

169

need your company, Bea, and I'm sure Kate will be grateful for your support. So let's stow your bike in the boot and I'll run you up to my house.'

Bea cheered up instantly. When she walked into Cory's living room where David was sitting reading the newspaper, he looked up and no amount of teasing could hide the pleasure in his eyes. 'Oh, so I'm still to put up with you then, am I?' he said.

Bea came back quickly with, 'If I can put up with you, you can put up with me. Anyway, you can't expect Dr Lawrence to cook for you, knowing what a fussy old so-and-so you are.'

'Blessed normality,' Kate sighed happily.

'They make such a lovely couple, don't they?' Cory chuckled.

'So devoted and loving,' Kate added, and for the second time that day they were laughing together. It made Kate feel very close to him and at the same time, very aware that he wasn't hers to feel close to.

As if to compound that fact Barbara arrived, letting herself in through the unlocked kitchen door. 'Is it a private party, or can anyone join in?' she called out cheerfully. Molly raced to greet her, but Barbara stopped her in her tracks with a glare and a sharp, 'Ladder these tights, lady, and you're in big trouble.' Molly, for once in her life, seemed to listen and take notice and Kate couldn't help feeling sorry for the exuberant little dog. Her tail went down flat and so did her ears. 'Aw, don't look at me like that,' Barbara said. 'I wouldn't do anything to hurt her. It's just that great daft lump is too soft with her and she needs a firm hand.'

'What have you got there?' Cory asked, stepping forward to take a suitcase from Barbara's hand. He kissed her cheek lightly.

'Clothes for Kate, of course,' Barbara said, rolling her eyes heavenwards. 'You can't expect her to go to work looking like a . . . a . . . '

'Clown?' Kate suggested.

'Exactly,' Barbara said. 'Come on, Kate. Let's go downstairs and I'll show you what I've brought.'

'Downstairs?' Bea looked puzzled.

'The downstairs is up and the upstairs is down,' David explained. 'We can sit outside on the veranda, which forms part of the roof for downstairs. It's a very interesting house.'

Cory carried the case downstairs and left the two women to unpack.

'I've brought you some shoes,' Barbara said. 'I know your feet are smaller than mine, but these were always a bit tight on me anyway and they'll do until you can get to the shops to get some in your own size. And there are some smart blouses and skirts, oh and a couple of nighties. And I stopped off and bought you some undies. Sophie opened the shop specially. And I've put in one or two personal items. I know it won't make up for what you've lost, Kate, but it'll tide you over until you can get your own things.' She broke off, startled to see Kate was in tears.

'What's wrong?'

'You've been so kind,' Kate wept, brushing her tears away only to have them quickly replaced by more. 'You and Cory, everyone.'

Barbara hugged her. 'It's what we do,' she said. 'And I know you'd do the same if it was me.'

★　★　★

Kate managed to sink herself into a fairly normal day at work. Everyone, it seemed, had heard of her predicament, and not a single patient came into her surgery without offering their condolences. Many also offered to help in any way they could.

The day sped by and Kate stifled a yawn as she cleared up her desk and prepared to go home. Home. It wasn't her home, she reminded herself, but Cory's.

There was a knock on her door and she called, 'Come in,' and expected to see Cory. The thud of disappointment when Geoffrey Blair poked his head round the door took her by surprise. 'Oh, Geoffrey,' she said, 'it's you.'

'Your carriage awaits,' he said cheerfully, oblivious to her disappointment. 'I'll drop you at Cory's house on my way home.'

'Thanks, Geoffrey, but Cory — '

'He's not here, my love,' Geoffrey told her with a twinkle in his eye. 'Called away on urgent business, so he asked me to see you safely home.'

'Safely home.' What did he think she was? A helpless little girl incapable of using her own two legs? Really, her anger was just a mask for her disappointment. She'd been looking forward to the ride home with Cory — more than she should have been; more than was sensible.

'You don't mind having a lift with Uncle Geoffrey do you?' Geoffrey asked, pretending to be offended. 'I promise to drive carefully, dib, dib, dib.'

Kate laughed at his comical expression and his clumsy attempt at a Boy Scout's salute. 'Geoffrey, it must be years since you wore a woggle.'

He assumed a wounded expression. 'I'll have you know, I was a jolly good Brownie.'

She slipped her arm through his and walked out into the corridor with him. 'So what was this urgent business?' she asked.

He tapped the side of his nose. 'Personal business,' he said.

'Nothing to do with a wedding, I suppose?' she muttered under her breath, but Geoffrey heard and for once in his life was struck dumb.

'No one is supposed to know about that,' he hissed. 'How did you find out?'

'Well, for goodness' sake, it's just a wedding isn't it?' she answered crossly. 'I don't know what the big deal is.'

Geoffrey grabbed her arm and steered her into the corner, well away from curious ears. 'The big deal is they want to arrange everything themselves. If it gets out that two of the town's most popular people are about to get spliced, Wyatt's Cove will probably set up a committee and turn it into the wedding of the year.'

'I'm sorry, Geoffrey,' she murmured, angry with herself for letting her temper get the better of her. 'It's been a long day.'

'Of course it has, my love,' Geoffrey said. 'But you have to put it all behind you now and start looking ahead.'

Ahead to what though? Kate thought dismally.

11

Kate arrived home to find her father all dressed up and ready to go out, but that couldn't be. She looked him up and down from his neatly pressed shirt to his gleaming shoes and she was stunned.

'Well?' he asked her. 'What do you think? Do I look all right?'

'Pa, you look terrific. What's happened?'

'I thought when I heard the car that it was my lift,' he said, wheeling his chair to the window and tugging the curtain aside.

'Your lift?' she babbled. 'What lift? Pa, will you tell me what's going on?'

But there was no time for at that moment, Bea's nippy little car pulled up outside. 'Bea?' Kate frowned as the older woman jumped out and all but skipped up the drive. 'You're looking very glamorous,' Kate remarked as she opened the door, but Bea brushed the compliment aside.

'Oh, go on with you. I look no different to usual. Are you ready, David?'

'You're late,' he accused.

'I said I'd pick you up around seven,' Bea retorted. 'I didn't say seven on the dot. Anyway, if all you're going to do is grump all evening, you can jolly well stay here and I'll find someone else to go with.'

His eyes crinkled as he smiled. 'You look lovely,' he said. 'For your age.'

'Oooh. I should push that wheelchair of yours right over the nearest cliff,' Bea cried, but the way her eyes were twinkling gave her away.

'Where are you going?' Kate asked, bemused.

'We're going to see a seaside show,' Bea told her. 'It's just a bit of fun and we could do with a laugh. I've heard the comedian is really good and I thought we needed cheering up after that rotten storm.'

Kate was baffled. Seaside shows were hardly her father's thing at all, but he was obviously looking forward to it.

'Don't look so perplexed, Kate.' David squeezed her arm. 'Bea won't really push me over the nearest cliff.'

Kate shook herself. He was going out — that was the important thing, and he was looking forward to it. Apparently he had no qualms about people looking at him or feeling sorry for him. He probably wouldn't dare; Bea wouldn't allow it.

'Come on then, let's go.' Bea grabbed his wheelchair and spun him round.

'Have a good time,' Kate said, and as she stooped to kiss her father goodbye, he caught her hand and held it tight.

'You and Cory will have this evening to yourselves,' he said urgently. 'Neither of you are on call. I checked.'

'So?'

'So make hay,' he said.

Kate flushed scarlet and Bea stepped to her rescue with a sharp, 'And I

thought you were coming to the show
to keep me company.'

'Get on with you, woman,' he replied.
'I spend all day with you. You don't
think I'd choose to spend all evening
with you as well, do you?'

'The feeling's mutual,' she retorted.
'You'd just better behave yourself,
that's all.'

Laughing, Kate helped Bea wheel
him out to the car and get him seated in
the passenger seat, then she folded the
chair and tried to get it in the boot. It
wouldn't fit.

'Curses!' Bea cried. 'Why on earth
didn't I think this through?' She bit her
lip and looked near to tears. Kate
looked at her father and saw that he
too, was looking bitterly disappointed.
She couldn't even come to the rescue
with her own car, as it was still parked
outside the bungalow, its keys lost
somewhere inside.

Suddenly struck by a flash of
inspiration, she said firmly, 'Stay where
you are. I'll phone the theatre and ask if

they have any wheelchairs.'

'Bound to have,' Bea cried, brightening. 'The town has won awards for being wheelchair friendly.'

Kate rushed into the house, made a quick phone call and returned a few moments later smiling all over her face. 'It's all arranged,' she said. 'Someone will meet you in the car park with a wheelchair. So you can go to the ball, Cinders.'

Far from looking pleased, her father just looked disgruntled. This time there was no humour lurking behind his grumpiness. Kate knew him well enough to know it was for real. She feared they'd lose him; that this small setback would knock him back miles.

'All this trouble,' he grumbled. 'I wish I'd just stayed home.'

Bea could see too that he wasn't joking, or even being jolly. She gave Kate a look, then walked briskly round to the driver's side and climbed in. 'You'd better cheer up,' she said. 'We're going to see a comedian and if you don't laugh, you won't get an ice cream in the interval.' Still he didn't smile and Bea, her voice edged with desperation, cried, 'For goodness sake, stop sitting there with a face like a cat's bottom and smile, man. You could at least pretend to like my company even if it is going to be an ordeal for you.'

His eyes widened as he turned to look at her. 'Is that what you think? Oh, Bea, I'm sorry.' His expression softened and he reached over to squeeze her hand.

Kate stepped back from the car, tears shimmering in her eyes. Not for the first time she suspected that underneath all that banter, there was very real affection. For while she had been carving out her own life here, something very special had been growing between David and Bea. She wondered if, when they were alone, there were many tender moments such as the one she had just witnessed. And it made her think too, that some of her father's depression might be due to guilt.

Bea started the engine and gave Kate a little wave, then pulled away. Through the open window, Kate heard her father say a little petulantly, 'What did you mean by that remark about a cat's bottom?'

Kate was still chuckling to herself as she went back into the house. Cory's house. Where was he now? Making last minute arrangements with Barbara for their wedding? Geoffrey was right about the pair of them being popular. Everywhere Kate went, people talked about Dr Cory and Nurse Barbara. She was on tenter-hooks waiting for him to come home and Molly was unsettled too, probably eager for a run. Kate looked out of the window. The windswept beach looked tempting and although she was tired, she felt the need to stretch her legs and get some fresh air into her lungs.

She found a navy-blue tracksuit among the clothes Barbara had loaned her and put it on, pleased with the fit.

She might not have Barbara's voluptuous curves, but they seemed to share a waist size.

'Come on, Molly,' she said. 'Come on, girl, let's go for a walk.'

Molly wheeled and bounded, yipping and yapping as Kate opened the kitchen door. Then the fast little dog shot out and ran ahead.

Kate followed at a more sedate pace, treading carefully down to the beach. Molly rushed up and down the sand, then spotted a flock of seagulls sitting on the beach and ran into them yipping wildly, sending them squawking into the sky. She was in and out of the water, leaping into the waves that broke feet from the shore, her energy seemingly endless.

Kate stopped for a moment, her hands plunged deep into the pockets of the tracksuit. Even the sky looked windswept with its smattering of small clouds, scudding so high above. A chilly breeze came off the sea as if it was chasing the storm.

The beach itself was littered with debris. Seaweed and driftwood lay in a line where the tide had thrown it. Kate drew in a deep breath, smelling the strong salty tang of the sea and remembered the day she was down here with Cory. The day he'd swept her up into his arms and carried her up to the house as if she weighed no more than a child. The memory was almost too painful to bear, yet it had been wonderful to be held in his arms and a part of her didn't want to forget, ever.

Molly crashed out of the waves and hurtled up the beach, then turned in a sharp circle, running nose to the ground, letting out silly little yaps as she went along. Her funny antics took Kate's mind off her own troubles and she ended up laughing out loud, her voice tossed away by the brisk wind.

At last she turned and headed for home. Molly wasn't running now, but trotting, her tongue lolling out as she panted. Far from feeling depressed and sad as she had when she'd come out,

Kate now felt exhilarated. The fresh air and laughter had done her the world of good.

But when she stepped back into the kitchen and saw Cory waiting for her, her high spirits plunged.

'You look lovely,' he said.

Kate blushed furiously and he held out a glass of wine. As she took it, his fingers brushed hers. Their eyes met and cymbals clashed inside Kate's head, making her feel dizzy. No, she told herself, this could not be happening.

And then he was turning away, his expression dark. 'Why don't you take your drink downstairs and get cleaned up,' he said briskly. 'Dinner's almost ready.'

'Dinner,' she breathed. 'Oh, I'm sorry, Cory. I planned to get us something. I didn't mean for you to come home and cook.'

'I'm used to it,' he said, keeping his back to her, but then he turned and his face lit with a grin. 'But I'll let you wash up. The dishwasher's on the blink.'

She reached for Molly's towel, but Cory took it from her and for one blissful, painful moment, their eyes locked as their hands brushed. They both pulled back as if they'd had a shock.

'I'll see to Molly,' he said. 'You can just get out of the way.'

'Sorry,' she mumbled. 'I'll go.' And she hurried downstairs.

He hadn't meant his voice to sound so harsh, and he could have kicked himself when he saw the look of hurt in her beautiful dark brown eyes. He began to rub the dog furiously with the towel, giving her the best drying she'd had in a long time.

Kate stood in front of the bathroom mirror staring at her reflection, horrified. Her hair was a tangled mess, her cheeks rosy red, her eyes bright. *No wonder he wanted me out of his kitchen,* she thought ruefully. *I look like an urchin.* She lifted the wineglass to her lips and swallowed the contents quickly, feeling it warm her all the way to her stomach.

She stripped off, turned on the shower then stepped beneath the hot, refreshing needles. She could wash off the sand, the salt, the smell of the sea, but she could never wash away the tingling she still felt when Cory's hand brushed hers.

After the shower she went in the bedroom and saw the wardrobe doors were open and her own things were hanging inside. Below them stood a neat row of her shoes. It was fantastic to have her own clothes back and she looked through, searching for something to wear. In the end, she opted for a white sundress with shoestring straps.

So that's why Cory was late home. That was the personal business he was attending to.

His eyes lit up briefly when he saw her, but very quickly the shades came down and she found it impossible to fathom what he must be thinking.

'You look beautiful,' he murmured.

Then with a visible effort, he pulled himself up. 'Sit down; it'll be ready soon. Are you hungry?'

'Famished.'

'Good. I've made enough risotto to feed an army. I'm not used to cooking for more than one.'

Kate sat and watched as he gave the rice concoction in the wok a last stir before moving it to the table. This was all so impossible. She couldn't look at him without her stomach turning somersaults or her pulses racing. He sat down and ladled the risotto onto two plates.

'Thanks for getting my things,' she said. 'It was good of you to take the trouble.'

He winced when she said that. 'Not at all,' he replied. 'I've got your car outside. I also fetched some of your father's belongings.' His tone had become almost formal.

'How did you manage?'

'With the help of my very good friend, Ben Chatterton. I doubt you've met him. He's our friendly neighbour-hood vet. He would have liked to have met you, but he had a previous engagement.'

Kate managed a weak smile and lifted a forkful of risotto to her lips. Surely Cory didn't have it in mind to pair her off with Ben Chatterton? The very idea! She pushed the thought to the back of her mind, dismissing it as too ridiculous for words.

'This is delicious, Cory,' she said.

The tension between them seemed to grow with every word spoken. Cory knew he'd have to do something to rescue the evening, or have it all fall down around his ears as a complete and utter disaster. He refilled her wineglass, ignoring her protests. 'You might need it when I tell you about the bungalow.'

Her eyes widened. 'What about it?'

'First the good news,' he said.

'Oh, there is good news?'

'Certainly.' He grinned. 'The bunga-low can be repaired. It's going to need some under-pinning and strengthening, but the foundations are very good. The rest is all fairly minor and the lot should be covered by your insurance. You are insured?'

'Yes, thank heaven.' She frowned, remembering what he'd said. 'You said the good news first. What's the bad?'

'It's going to take several months.'

'Months!' she cried, dismayed.

'Now hold on, don't go getting all het up. You want the job done properly, don't you? Well it all takes time. You'll have to get estimates, then get them okayed by the insurers.'

'And in the meantime, we impose on your hospitality,' she murmured. 'Oh, Cory, this is such a mess. I'm so sorry about all this. First thing tomorrow, I'll see if I can find somewhere to rent.'

'At this time of year?' He laughed. 'Anyway, what's wrong with here? I like having you, your father feels at home here, and Molly . . . ' He broke off and looked down at the dog sitting beside him, her tail swishing backwards and forwards across the floor. 'What can I say? Molly here thinks it's all incredibly exciting.'

Kate had mixed feelings, very mixed feelings. She was happy that the bungalow could be saved, and glad Cory wanted her to stay on here, but could she really cope living in the same house as him for months? She'd considered applying for another position, but that could take forever, and would her father be keen to leave Wyatt's Cove now that he'd formed such a close friendship with Bea? Thinking of the pair of them cheered her up considerably. She just hoped that everything had gone well and they were having a great time.

'Penny for them?' Cory said.

She looked up and he was gazing at her with that odd, faraway look in his eyes. They were very dark tonight with bright rims, like storm clouds hiding a golden sun.

'I was thinking about Pa,' she said.

'Yes, I'd been wondering about him.' Cory grinned. 'I gathered he'd gone out somewhere, but I must admit, the wheelchair in the hall had me foxed.'

Kate explained quickly about not being able to get the wheelchair into Bea's boot and found herself relaying the exchanges between David and Bea.

He threw back his head and laughed. 'It seems to me that Bea is all the medicine your father needs.'

They chatted about all kinds of subjects as they cleared away the dinner things. He steered clear of talking about Kate and she was glad. Maybe he'd given up trying to figure her out. She hoped so, and yet she didn't.

'Let's go and sit outside,' he said. 'It's a perfect evening.'

'Sounds good to me,' Kate said. 'What a difference to last night.'

Everywhere had that scrubbed, empty look that so often follows a storm and there was a stiff breeze, but it was very pleasant. They sat down on the swing seat and Cory gently rocked them with his foot. The motion of the seat was relaxing and comforting and Kate leaned back and closed her eyes.

It took Cory a moment or two to realise she'd fallen asleep. He looked down at her, loving that her face had relaxed in sleep and she didn't have those little worry lines on her forehead. David had told him how she'd been hurt by a former boyfriend. They'd talked at great length about Kate. He couldn't imagine how anyone could be stupid enough to let her go.

At last she stirred and sat up. 'What time is it?' she asked sleepily.

'Almost ten. I wonder how your dad is getting on.'

She chuckled softly. 'Arguing with Bea about who should buy the ice creams, I shouldn't wonder.'

'I think she's really rather fond of him,' Cory said. 'Don't you? And vice versa. From what I've seen of your father, he wouldn't tolerate anyone he didn't like.'

'She's worked miracles getting him to go out at all,' she said. Her face was bathed in the soft glow of the outside light and she looked up at him from beneath her thick, dark lashes. 'And you worked a miracle too, Cory. Thank you. I think you're probably the first fellow doctor who has treated him like another human being and not a patient.'

'It seems the only medicine he needed was to see you happy,' Cory remarked. She flushed. Perhaps he was right. But how long could they keep up the pretence that they were in love? And when they stopped, would it set David back knowing he'd been duped? After all, Cory couldn't keep his forthcoming marriage to Barbara a secret forever.

'Now we have to start thinking about you. What medicine do you need, Kate?' He tilted her chin and gave in to the urge he'd been fighting all evening and kissed her. She stiffened, trying to quell everything in her that longed to respond, but in the end her will was useless against his and she melted into his arms.

12

Kate was lost, her senses reeling.

Somehow, through the mist in her mind, she came brutally to her senses. How could he be kissing her when he was supposed to be in love with Barbara? How could he even think of deceiving her? Kate made a conscious effort to pull herself together.

But before she could summon the will to push him away, he'd drawn away from her and instead of feeling relieved, Kate felt nothing but a crushing sense of disappointment and hurt.

He couldn't bring himself to look her in the eye. It had taken every ounce of willpower he possessed to stop this madness now, but stop it he must. 'I think you should go to bed,' he said hoarsely.

'But I . . . ' She looked so bewildered

and lost; it was all he could do not to gather her up in his arms again.

'Do as I ask, Kate — please.'

Kate scrambled to her feet. 'I'm sorry,' she stammered, humiliation burning inside her.

'It's getting late,' he told her. 'We've both had too much to drink and if you stay here with me, I don't think I . . . Just go, Kate, please. For goodness sake, go.'

She turned and ran, blinded by tears down the stairs to her room where she flung herself down on the bed and wept.

She'd never felt like this before, not even with Gareth, and it threatened to overwhelm her now. How could she live with it? How could she live with herself?

Tonight, all of it, was one big, stupid mistake.

She'd almost stopped crying when she heard Cory's footsteps on the stairs, but it was too late for her to wipe her tears away. Her breath lodged in her throat as he rushed in, his hair tousled, his eyes shining. He looked at her for a moment and it was as if he was speared with pain. She'd seen him wince like that before and wondered how much it had to do with Barbara and the time he'd so nearly lost her. Did it haunt him still?

When he finally spoke, his voice was abrupt. 'I'm going to need your help, Kate. There's been an explosion on a boat down at the marina and there are several casualties. Ambulances are on the way.'

She jumped to her feet at once. 'Will we take them to our hospital?' she asked as she raced up the stairs behind him.

'I think there are some serious burns. They'll have to go straight to the specialist burns unit. Until we get there, I don't know what the picture is.'

He didn't speak as he drove them across town to the small marina, where a team of firemen was already tackling the blaze raging on board one of the small craft.

'Geoffrey's already here,' he muttered. 'It's just a shame we couldn't get hold of Barbara. She's great in this kind of emergency.'

Kate and Cory dealt with an array of different injuries. The confusion was terrible. As the firefighters tried to douse the flames, the medics dealt with the casualties, some of them more badly hurt than others.

'I'm going in the ambulance with this one,' Geoffrey called out as the worst burns victim was carried carefully on board.

All in all, it was a traumatic couple of hours. Kate had never been in a situation like it before, but she put her own feelings aside and worked calmly and efficiently under tremendous pressure.

'That's about the lot then,' Cory said as they closed the ambulance doors and watched it race away with the last patient. The fire was almost out, the rest of the boats out of immediate danger.

Kate was still reeling a little and now it was over, she could feel herself trembling. Cory rested his arm gently across her shoulders. 'You all right, Kate?' She nodded.

'Doctors, over here! We've found another one.'

Kate and Cory both ran behind the fireman to the jetty and beyond to where the shore dipped into a sandy beach.

'She's down here,' he told them. 'On the beach. She must have been thrown there by the force of the explosion.'

'Have we got any light?' Cory called.

'I'll sort it out for you, Doc. She's in a bad way.'

'It's all right, love,' Kate said, kneeling on the sand beside the woman. 'You're going to be all right now.' It was hard to see in the darkness.

'Were you on the boat?' Cory asked. He shrugged off his jacket and covered her with it. 'What's your name, love?'

'Marjorie,' the woman whispered

weakly. 'Please, you have to find Penny.'

'Is Penny your dog?'

'Yes, she just took off. She was so frightened. It was such a big blast. My ears are still ringing. You must find Penny.'

'We'll find her,' Cory said.

'What sort of dog is she?' Kate asked.

'Cocker spaniel.'

The firemen arrived on the scene. Then they aimed a spotlight onto the sand, bathing the whole area in brilliance. Kate flinched and shielded her eyes.

'She's probably made her way home,' Kate assured her. 'She'll be there waiting for you.'

'But Penny's such a nervous dog.'

'We'll sort something out, don't worry about her,' Kate assured her and looked across at Cory, who was busy setting up a drip.

'Oh, it's you, Dr Lawrence.' Marjorie seemed to brighten up. 'I didn't realise.'

'Hello, Marjorie,' he said, smiling warmly. 'What were you doing out on the beach so late at night?'

'Trouble sleeping,' Marjorie said. 'Penny doesn't like loud noises. Poor little thing, she'll be terrified.'

'Have you had her long?'

There was no reply.

'Marjorie,' Kate said. 'Stay with us.'

'It's all right, dear,' Marjorie whispered. 'I'm not going anywhere.'

Kate squeezed her hand and repeated her question about the dog.

'How old did you say Penny was?' Cory asked. 'Marjorie. How old is Penny?'

'Five years,' Marjorie said. 'She's still a pup at heart though. She's a mad little thing.'

'Typical spaniel.' Cory smiled.

The three of them carried on chatting as if they'd simply met on the beach, with Marjorie slipping in and out of consciousness, until at last a siren could be heard.

'You will take care of her for me, won't you?' Marjorie whispered, her voice barely audible.

'Until you're better, of course we will,' Kate said.

'Thank you. Thank you both.'

'Here they are at last,' Cory said. 'We'll soon have you safe, love.'

Marjorie reached out and grasped Cory's arm. 'I've done a lot of thinking while I've been lying here helpless,' she said. 'I'm going to move in with my daughter. She's been asking me for ages, but I wouldn't because of Penny. But now . . . '

'Ah, so Penny's the reason,' he said.

'I didn't tell you before because I thought you'd think I was daft,' she said.

'Of course I don't think that,' he said. 'I'd feel exactly the same way. But don't make any hasty decisions about the future.'

'It's not a hasty decision,' she said. 'I've been thinking about it for a long time. But I'll only do it if I can find a good home for Penny. My daughter is allergic to dogs, you see.'

'Don't worry, Marjorie,' Kate said.

203

'We'll sort something out.'

As the paramedics carried her away, Kate turned to Cory. 'She'll be all right,' she said gently, resting her hand on his shoulder.

He stood, clenching his fists at his sides, his temple twitching. 'But she might not have been,' he said, his voice sounding terribly hollow. 'What if she hadn't been found?'

'But she was!'

Geoffrey had returned and hurried over to them. A deep frown creased Cory's forehead and his brows knotted together as if he was suffering from some sort of delayed shock. He must have been in much worse situations than this, Kate thought, many times if he'd been working in a disaster zone. Then she banished the thought, furious with herself. He should be used to it — that was what she'd almost thought, but she knew in her heart that it was something you never got used to. Oh, you could harden your heart and hide your feelings, but underneath you were still a human being with human emotions.

'Cory, where are you going?' She took a step towards him, but he backed away, holding up his hands palms outwards.

'No, Kate. I need to be on my own for a while. I'll see you in a minute.'

She watched him walk away along the dark beach, his wide shoulders hunched, and her heart ached for him. He looked so terribly alone, and then he was out of sight.

Geoffrey leaned forward and whispered gruffly, 'Don't worry about Cory. He'll be all right.'

★   ★   ★

It wasn't the first time Cory had found himself raging at his own helplessness. You tried to play God, but in the end, you were just a man and there were times when that just wasn't good enough. This time it had been okay, but there had been times in the past when it hadn't.

Kate had coped amazingly well. She was very cool under pressure. He thought of her standing there on the sand beside Geoffrey, her pretty white dress blackened with smoke, her face grimy.

He'd gone along the darkened beach, wrestling with his thoughts for some distance, when he heard a whimper. At first he thought it was simply a product of his own imagination, then he realised it was very real and very close.

'Penny?' he said softly. 'Penny, is that you?'

He followed the sound of the whimpering and found the little dog cowering behind the rocks. It was hard to see in the darkness, but as he reached out and touched her he could feel she was trembling. She growled softly, her warning coming from her fear.

'It's all right, girl, I won't hurt you,' he said, gently coaxing, softly talking until he had won her trust. It took some time before she stopped whining and crept out from behind the rocks. He knew he'd cracked it when he felt her hot tongue lick his hand. Carefully, in case she was injured, he lifted her into his arms and carried her quickly back along the beach towards the emergency lights.

Marjorie had told him several times how her daughter had asked her to go and live with her, and he'd said she should consider it. She said there was a very good reason she couldn't, but she wouldn't tell him what it was. And now he held the reason in his arms — this lovely little dog.

Marjorie was an amazing lady who coped with her many ailments with never a word of complaint, but her life would be so much easier if she lived with her daughter. Penny licked his face and he could feel her little tail wagging like mad.

As the jetty came clearly into view, he saw a lone figure standing on the boards some little distance from where the clearing-up operation was

207

in progress, the skirt of her dress billowing softly around her legs. His heart leapt at the sight of her and he would have given anything to be able to run to her, hold her in his arms, and soothe away all their combined pain.

Instead, as he drew level, he said, 'I found the dog.'

'So I see.' She reached out to fondle the little dog's ears. 'I promised Marjorie I'd make sure she was taken care of if we found her,' Kate said, for the first time showing any shred of emotion. 'Thinking about re-homing Penny must have been such a hard decision. We will take care of Penny, won't we, Cory?'

'Of course we will, love,' he said, her sudden weakness making him feel strong and fully in control. 'Of course we will.'

13

Bea opened the door and was visibly shocked at the sight of the pair of them as they walked in. They were bedraggled, their faces blackened and sooty, their clothes — particularly Kate's — stained with blood.

'What on earth happened?' she cried. 'You look dreadful.'

'Where's my dad?' Kate asked.

'I helped him to bed ages ago,' Bea replied. 'We heard there'd been a bad accident down at the marina and guessed that was where you were. I said I'd stay here until you were home.'

Molly rushed out and slowed right down, a suspicious gleam in her eyes when she saw that Cory held another dog in his arms. She stopped dead, one paw raised as she sniffed the air.

'Gently, Molly,' Cory instructed as he put the other dog down. 'Gently, girl.'

For once in her life, Molly did exactly as she was told, as if some sixth sense told her all that this other little dog had been through.

Cory straightened up and ran his hand back through his hair. 'Molly's never been what you'd call territorial. She'll probably be only too pleased to have a companion.'

The dogs circled each other warily, then Molly licked Penny's face and both tails, one short and stumpy, the other long and feathery, began to twitch in friendship.

'That's Penny, isn't it?' Bea remarked. 'Marjorie Bennett's little dog.'

Kate and Cory exchanged looks and Bea's lips tightened.

'She's all right,' Kate said quickly. 'She's been taken to hospital, but she'll be fine.'

'Oh, thank goodness,' Bea said, holding her hand to her heart. 'What about the dog? What will happen to her?'

'Penny will be staying with us,' Cory

said. 'This is her home now, and of course Marjorie can come and visit her any time when she's better.'

A little later, when Bea had gone home, Cory rested his hands on Kate's shoulders. 'Thanks for waiting for me on the beach,' he said.

'You weren't the only one who needed a bit of time to think, you know.' She laughed lightly in an attempt to hide her embarrassment, but it contained no humour. The last thing she wanted him to think was that she cared. 'I was giving you a few minutes, then I was going to take one of the rescuers up on his offer of a lift.'

'Oh, I see,' he said, then dropped a brief, soft kiss on her forehead before sending her away downstairs to bed.

In the morning David was up bright and early, having made friends with the new arrival before Kate had even surfaced. She felt like death warmed up. Two bad nights on the trot and she was absolutely shattered.

A great change had come over Molly.

She seemed to sense Penny's nervousness and was calmer and quieter. Even though she was the younger of the dogs, having Penny there seemed to bring out all her maternal instincts.

'Did you have a good night last night, Pa?' she asked, remembering that he'd been out with Bea and that it was something of a milestone in his recovery. It would be wrong to overlook his achievements because of what happened.

'Better than yours,' he said sadly. 'Cory said there were some pretty bad injuries.'

'Yes,' Kate said woodenly. 'If we'd got there sooner . . . '

'If, if, if.' David shook his head sadly. 'Don't even try to blame yourself. Getting there sooner would have made no difference. Look at the positives of what you did do. You saved lives and no one died. You can't ask for more than that. And that lady — Marjorie, was it? Cory had a call this morning to say she's doing better than expected and will be allowed to go home with her daughter in a day or two.'

'Where is Cory?'

'He left some time ago. Took the dogs for a long walk, then went. Kate, he said if you didn't feel up to going in this morning, he'd understand. He said that he and Geoffrey would see your patients.'

'Of course I'm going in,' she said. 'Will you be all right on your own until Bea comes?'

He made a noise of irritation. 'I'm not a child, Kate. I'm perfectly capable of taking care of myself. But you haven't had breakfast.'

'I can't face it, Pa,' she said.

It was the usual mixed bag of patients. Kate dispensed with her morning surgery fairly briskly and got through her home visits by lunchtime. Just as she was about to grab a sandwich, she was called to the hospital, where one of her patients produced a healthy four-kilo baby boy. It cheered up what would otherwise have been a pretty bleak day.

Before afternoon surgery, she had a brief conference with the district nurse, then prepared herself for the usual round of tummy bugs, throat infections and hay fever.

With the health centre relatively quiet, except for the distant hum of the vacuum cleaner, Kate got on with some paperwork, catching up with her correspondence until she realised the place was really silent and time had marched on. *Time to call it a day,* she thought as she stood and stretched her aching limbs. She closed the door to her surgery and heard the sound of muted voices behind Cory's door. A prickle of unease had the hairs at the nape of her neck standing on end. Cory wasn't staying late tonight, was he? She crept forward, heart hammering, and pushed the door slightly ajar so she could look in.

And there was Barbara, nestling in Cory's strong arms, resting her head against his broad chest. Kate let out an involuntary cry before she could stop herself.

'Kate! What is it?' Cory released Barbara and moved towards her.

'Kate?' Barbara was coming towards her as well, both of them wearing expressions of concern. 'Are you all right? You're as white as a sheet.'

'I heard voices,' Kate rushed out her explanation. 'I thought we were being burgled.'

Barbara gave her a smile, then reached out and took Cory's hand. 'Thanks, Cory,' she said. 'I knew I could rely on you.'

'You can always do that, Barbara,' he said with genuine affection.

Barbara turned to Kate and with a wry smile said, 'I've managed to persuade him to wear top hat and tails on the big day. It took some doing, I'll tell you.'

Kate did her best to ignore the pain she felt and mustered a smile. 'I'll bet.'

'Goodnight, then,' Barbara went on.

'Time I was leaving too,' Kate said

quickly, having no wish to be left alone here with Cory.

'Hold on just a minute, Kate,' Cory said. 'Sit down.'

Reluctantly she sank onto the chair. 'Will this take long?'

'It's about your father,' he said. 'He's been to the day centre today, asking Denise about physiotherapy and so on. He's determined to beat this thing, Kate, and I think he can do it. There's nothing keeping him in that chair apart from wasted muscles and no will to get out of it.'

'That's not true,' she cried. 'Pa's spine was damaged in the accident.'

'Yes, it was, but tests have shown that the damage wasn't permanent. There's no reason on this earth why, given time and patience, your father shouldn't walk again. He'll always have limited use of his arms and his concentration is such that he'll never practice as a doctor again, but he can have a life of his own, Kate. A good life.'

It took her a few moments to digest

all this. While her father was forging ahead in leaps and bounds, she, it seemed, was getting left behind.

'So you see,' Cory went on gently, 'you don't have to plan your life around him. If he has a life of his own, then so can you.' He rose and came around the desk, reaching towards her. How could he, when a few moments ago he'd been holding Barbara, his fiancée?

She scrambled out of the chair and backed away from him. She was scared, not of Cory but of herself, and she liked Barbara far too much to let anything happen. 'Thank you for letting me know,' she said coolly. 'I think I should go now.'

He looked close to despair. 'What is it, Kate? If it's about last night . . . '

'I've seen people with bad injuries before.'

'I'm not talking about that. I'm talking about what happened before. You and me.'

'There is no you and me, Cory,' she cried angrily. 'I had too much to drink and made a fool of myself, end of story.'

'You didn't make a fool of yourself,' he said raggedly. 'If anyone did that, then it was me.'

He tried to hold her, but she squirmed away, desperate to avoid having him touch her; knowing that if he did, all her carefully composed resolve would dissolve. 'Don't touch me,' she said. 'Please.'

He dropped his hands to his sides in a gesture of defeat. 'I won't be home for dinner tonight,' he said, turning away and pretending to be engrossed with something on his desk. 'I'm due at a meeting of the Summer Gala Committee. It's an annual event organised by the Hospital Friends. Do you want to come along?'

'Still trying to integrate me into the community?' she asked, the depth of her own unhappiness making her sound bitter.

'I thought you might find it interesting, that's all.'

'I promised Pa . . . '

Suddenly all Cory's control seemed to drain away. 'You could stop babying him, Kate. He's a grown man and he has his pride and dignity. How do you think it makes him feel, having you stopping in all the time to be with him? Do you think he doesn't realise?'

'He gets lonely,' she said, her voice small.

'You're making him lonely. You've got to stop coddling him, Kate. I know you've done everything you can for him these past four years, but you've gone too far, allowing him to accept his lot.'

She couldn't believe what she was hearing. Did Cory blame her for her father's condition? But wasn't there a grain of truth in what he said? She tried to deny it, but couldn't, not if she were to be brutally honest with herself.

'I'm sorry,' she said at last. 'I have other things to do.'

'Just stop using your father as an excuse for not living your own life. You're not being fair on him.' He dropped his voice and looked at her from beneath his sooty lashes. 'And you're not being fair on yourself.'

Back home Kate found her father in a buoyant mood, determined to tell her about the show the night before. 'Marvellous young comedian,' he enthused. 'He had us in stitches. We had a wonderful time, then we went to the West Cliff Hotel for a meal. Bea's right about the town being wheelchair-friendly. Everywhere we went I was treated with respect, and no one treated me like an oddity.'

'Well, that's because you're not an oddity, Pa,' Kate said with a smile.

'You should go and see him. He's here for the season,' he told her. 'Perhaps Cory would take you.'

What a mess this is, Kate thought. There was her father getting better, making real progress for the first time, and she should have been rejoicing. Instead she was worrying that they'd have to move. But if they stayed around here, Cory would marry Barbara and all David's illusions would be shattered anyway.

'I hear you've been to the day centre,' she said, changing the subject adroitly.

To her further amazement, he was just as enthusiastic about that as he was about the comedian. 'Denise Blair is terrific,' he said. 'A real tonic. She said the same as Cory, that I should take up swimming again. I won't ever regain the full use of my arms, but I can strengthen them and make what use I do have more effective.'

Kate stroked both dogs that had come to greet her. Molly was definitely in charge, this being her house, but Penny seemed quite happy to follow her lead. David called to the smaller dog and she went over to him, sitting at his feet while he stroked her soft head.

'Cory double-checked with Marjorie and she definitely wants to re-home Penny,' he said, then added with a smile, 'So it looks as if we've got ourselves a dog. I've had the vet, Ben, come out and check her over, just in case. Cory thought she might have been hurt by the blast, but Ben says she's fine.'

'Ben?' Kate looked puzzled. What else was going on in her father's life that she didn't know about?

'Ben Chatterton.' He chuckled infuriatingly and added enigmatically, 'We're old friends, didn't I tell you?'

And if Kate thought the surprises would end there, she was mistaken, for no sooner had he told her that he was friends with the vet, than he was going on to say, 'And tomorrow Bea and I are off round the town. We'll be taking a picnic lunch and making a day of it.'

Kate was pleased — of course she was — but if her father was going out for the day, that meant she'd be home alone with Cory, and she wasn't sure if she could stand it.

14

The next morning, Kate stood outside Cory's house waving goodbye to her father and Bea as they set off on their trek around the town.

'If I get tired, I'll phone you to come and collect us,' Bea said.

'Do that,' Kate told her. 'Have fun. Enjoy yourselves.'

It was a glorious sunny day with a refreshing breeze coming in off the sea. Cory stood beside Kate, his arm casually draped around her shoulders, keeping up the pretence that they were a couple. It was becoming wearying, especially as they both knew it was such a sham.

The moment the wheelchair disappeared, Cory took his arm away; and as they went back into the house, the inches between them might just as well have been miles.

'I'm taking the dogs along the beach. Want to come?' he asked.

'No thank you,' she replied primly.

'It doesn't have to be like this, Kate.'

'Doesn't it?'

'Of course not.'

She was almost lulled by his soft, persuasive voice and she knew if she allowed herself to look in his beautiful dark eyes she'd be completely lost. As it was, she could feel her resolve weakening as he took her in his arms.

'I can't bear this atmosphere between us, Kate,' he said. 'It's tearing me apart. I don't know where we went wrong, but couldn't we try again?'

Try again. She came to her senses and tried to wriggle free, but his hold on her was firm and struggling useless.

'You must realise how I feel about you,' he said. 'And I'm sure you feel the same way.'

'Don't be ridiculous,' she cried and began to wriggle again. 'Let me go.'

'And if I won't?' His eyes glittered

with the challenge. 'What will you do then, Kate?'

Kate had never felt so torn, so utterly wrenched apart by her own feelings. The storm that had raged inside her for so long was coming to a head. 'Just let me go!'

'Do you really hate me so much, Kate?' he asked her, his voice roughened.

'No, but you're making me want to hate you,' she replied softly.

He released her then and backed away. 'I'm sorry,' he said. 'I've obviously been reading you wrong all this time. It seems I've been making a complete fool of myself. I thought we had something . . . ' He looked so hurt, she longed to reach out and hold him and tell him that no, he hadn't been wrong. She loved him, heart and soul.

'But don't worry,' he said bitterly. 'I won't make the same mistake again.' Then he turned on his heel, called to the dogs and strode out of the house. Kate rushed to the window to watch his descent down the steps, his long, lean legs carrying him ever further away. She felt as if her heart was breaking in two.

She stayed at the window, watching as he reached the shore and walked along the water's edge, the dogs bounding and bouncing around him. He stooped, picked up a stone and sent it flying out to sea. There had been something so angry about the gesture. Maybe it was psychological; maybe he wished it was Kate he could fling away.

But he had it coming, she reminded herself. *It's his own fault, the two-timing rat.* Yet no matter how hard she tried, she couldn't find it in her to hate him or even be angry with him.

When he was out of sight, she went downstairs and carefully packed away the clothes Barbara had loaned her. She had to get away, and this was the perfect excuse.

Barbara lived in one of the tall terraces on the seafront overlooking the promenade. The house had been painted a soft shade of pink. 'Kate.

How nice to see you.' Barbara smiled when she answered the door. She was wearing a silk robe tied loosely around her slim waist and her black hair, normally so neat, was tousled and tumbling about her shoulders. 'I've only just got up.'

'I'm sorry,' Kate said, flustered. 'I just brought your things back.'

'Don't be sorry,' Barbara said. 'Come in and have some coffee. I've just made it, so it's fresh and it's decent stuff, not like that rubbish we have at the health centre. But that's Cory for you; he'd rather spend money on the patients than the staff.'

'Is that such a bad thing?' Kate asked, and her tone was gritty and irritable.

'What's wrong with you this morning, Kate?' Barbara said. 'Did you get out on the wrong side of the bed?' She laughed. She could be abrupt and a little cold at times, not to mention bitchy, but underneath she had a warm heart. Kate even found herself wishing she had some of Barbara's strength — or maybe it was just her man she wanted.

'Come on through. We'll sit in the kitchen; it's the best room in the house at this time of day.'

Kate followed her through to a large sunny kitchen where several cats lounged in various pools of sunshine. One of them stirred and yawned, and Kate tickled its ears before going to stand at the window which overlooked a long terraced garden.

'What a lovely house,' she said.

'Mmm, it is,' Barbara murmured. 'One day I'm going to fill it to the rafters with children.'

Kate turned to look at her and was astonished to see that Barbara was blushing. 'Oh, I know I don't look the type, but I'm in my mid-thirties now and I know the biological clock is ticking away a little faster every year. I'd like to have lots of children, more than four, but I know at my age two is probably a more sensible target.'

'So you're going to live here after you're married?'

'Of course.' Barbara looked puzzled. 'Where on earth else would we live? Come and have your coffee, Kate.'

Kate sat down on a stool. 'There are still some clothes in the wash. I'll iron them before I bring them back.'

'Oh, no hurry,' Barbara said with a dismissive wave of her hand. 'I've loads of clothes. It's my weakness.' She looked thoughtful for a moment, then her lovely almond eyes turned to Kate and she said, 'It must have been an awful shock for you, waking up with your house falling down around your ears.'

Kate chuckled. 'It wasn't quite like that, Barbara.' Then she became more serious and added, 'I think it was worse afterwards, when I thought about what could have happened.'

Barbara nodded sympathetically. 'I know exactly what you mean. All the time Cory and I were in China I was fine, but when we got home it all hit me. Cory made me have counselling. If it wasn't for him, goodness knows where I would have ended up. He saved my life out there and he saved it again back home. It's always the aftermath, isn't it? Delayed shock can be the worst kind to cope with.'

For a moment, both women looked glum and gloomy. It was Barbara who suddenly straightened up and said, 'Listen to us. What a morbid pair. We should take a leaf out of your father's book and enjoy ourselves instead of dwelling on the past.'

'My father?'

'Oh, yes. He enjoyed the show the other night. I know it was only an unknown young comedian in a rather tacky little theatre, but it was a riot.'

'You were there?'

'Mmm. He's a lovely man, your dad. The lady with him — Bea, wasn't it? Yes, she was having fun too. They get on really well together, don't they?'

Kate laughed ruefully. 'She won't stand any nonsense from him and she puts up with his bad moods.'

'Hopefully his moods will lighten as he comes out of himself more. Perhaps we could get him involved with the Gala. We had a meeting about it last night and we could always use extra people on the committee.'

'You were there?' Kate gulped. Of course she was. She and Cory were a pair, weren't they? Even if they were trying to keep quiet about just how serious their relationship was.

'Of course. I have to be seen to support my man, even if I would rather sit at home with my feet up,' she laughed lightly. 'It wouldn't do you any harm to join in, too.'

'I thought it was supposed to be a big secret,' Kate remarked.

'The wedding is, yes. We've been an item for so long, I think people probably forget we're not already married.'

Kate finished her coffee and looked at her watch. 'I have to go.'

Barbara got to her feet and walked

Kate to the door. 'If you come to call again, and I do hope you will, you know you can walk round the beach from Cory's house? Just don't bring that delinquent hound with you. Last time Cory brought her here, she nearly wrecked the place, and she upset my cats. It's a nice walk as long as you make sure the tide's well out. Cory and I discovered it shortly after I moved here.'

'I bet you did,' Kate snapped, then smiled to take the sting out of her words. Barbara seemed not to notice. *She's a nice woman,* Kate thought. *It isn't her fault I've fallen for Cory.*

'I hope Penny's settled down,' Barbara added as Kate walked away.

'She has,' Kate said, gritting her teeth. So Cory had already told Barbara about Penny. What else had he told her? Not about the way he'd been pursuing her, that was for sure.

On the way back to Cory's house she took a detour, driving herself to the part of the town which had been set aside as a nature reserve. She parked the car and walked through the long grass to the point where she finally sat, hugging her knees, gazing across the water. Below her the cliff fell away, steep and relentless, to a sandy cove. On the face of the cliff fulmars sat on their nests, shielding their young from the prevailing wind.

'I could stay here forever,' Kate said out loud. 'I love this place.' It felt good to say it out loud. She shivered. Yes, she did love it already. It was a wonderful place, small and probably unimportant, but it had something about it so that once you lived here, it got in your blood. Her heart was here and no matter how loud the voice inside her head told her she should move on, before it was too late, she wasn't listening.

15

Kate was on her way home from the headland when she saw Cory's car heading towards her. She slowed down and as she passed, he waved to her to stop, then pulled in further along the road.

By the time she'd parked and got out of her car, he was running towards her and Kate's heart was pounding behind her ribs. What did he want? Had something happened to her father?

'Where have you been?' he demanded furiously. 'What were you doing up here on your own?'

'I went to see Barbara, then I explored a little. I really don't know why you're so worried.'

'Of course I'm worried, Kate.' His voice was rough; whether with tenderness or anger, Kate couldn't tell. 'You've been through a lot.'

'How many times do I have to tell

you? I'm perfectly all right.'

'I don't agree.'

'Is that your medical opinion, Doctor?' Her heart was banging erratically behind her ribs, but there was nothing in her cool façade to show the turbulence she felt inside. Was it going to be like this every time she saw him, or would the symptoms fade and die in time?

'I can't help that I care about you, Kate.' He ran his hand back through his thick windswept hair with frustration. 'It tears me apart when I see all that fear and sadness in your eyes.'

She turned away. Was she really so transparent? Cory watched her closely. When she hadn't come home, he'd looked everywhere he could think of for her. He'd been tearing himself apart ever since, wondering where she'd gone.

'Look, Cory, it's getting late. I haven't had any lunch and I'm absolutely ravenous. Do you mind if I go now?'

'Mind?' His voice was husky. 'Of course I don't mind. You go ahead and I'll follow. I haven't eaten either, so perhaps we could have something together.'

She stiffened.

'It's all right, Kate,' he said bitterly. 'I'm only asking you to have lunch with me. I won't make the mistake of kissing you again.'

She was almost home when she spotted Bea pushing David along in his chair. The poor woman looked all in and her face lit up when Kate pulled up alongside.

'Want a lift?'

'Oh, please,' Bea breathed. 'I think I've overdone it a bit. We've been miles, haven't we, David?'

'I think we must have covered every inch of this place,' he replied wearily. 'It's been great, though tough on poor Bea.'

Kate got out just as Cory pulled up behind them. 'Want a hand?'

'I'll drive back with Cory,' David said immediately. 'You girls can go together in Kate's car.'

'Girls!' Bea laughed.

Kate raised no objection and within minutes, they were all back at Cory's house.

'I hope you don't mind, Kate,' David said once they were all inside. 'But Bea has invited me to spend the day at her cottage tomorrow. I said I'd give her a hand in her greenhouse.'

'Of course I don't mind, Pa.' Kate gave him a hug and rumpled his thinning hair with her hand. 'But don't feel you have to go out on my account. Cory and I don't have any plans.'

'Well, I think I'd like to lie down for a while now,' he said, stifling a yawn. 'All that fresh air and sunshine has made me weary. Would you mind, Cory?'

Cory went at once with David, pushing him through to the bedroom and leaving Kate and Bea alone.

'It's so long since I've seen him this happy,' Kate said. 'Thank you.'

'Don't thank me,' Bea said quickly. 'I'm not just doing it for him. I've been having a wonderful time, too. He's a lovely man and he makes me feel useful and important again. When my husband was alive we used to run a small hotel, and I've often thought my biggest mistake was giving it up. But you make the decisions in the midst of your grief and when you look back, it's too late to change them. To be truthful, I applied for the job as your housekeeper because I thought taking care of someone worse off than myself would be good for me. How wrong I was. I couldn't feel sorry for your father if I tried. He'd never allow it anyway.'

'You really enjoy his company, don't you?' Kate said.

'Yes, I do. And I think, despite all he says, that he enjoys mine, too.'

Much later, in the early evening, Cory cooked food on the barbecue and the three of them sat out in the garden. Cory's mood was serious and sombre and Kate found she missed his teasing, but knew in her heart that the time for all that was over. Their relationship had entered a new phase. She'd left him in no doubt as to her feelings. She refused to feel sorry for him. He'd brought it all on himself.

Despite his lengthy afternoon nap, Kate's father was soon tired, and he asked her to help him to bed. 'What's happened?' he asked, once they were inside. 'Have you and Cory fallen out?'

'Not exactly,' she replied and tried to compose her face into an expression that would fool her father. 'Maybe we're just not suited.'

'Not suited? I've never seen two people who went so well together,' David said. 'He's obviously crazy about you and you're in love with him, so what's the problem? It's not still me, is it, Kate? Oh, surely it's not me.'

'Of course it's not you, Pa,' she laughed. 'Why, we'll get you through your MOT this year with no problems and you'll be striding off into the sunset with Bea on your arm.'

'You might not be so far off the mark there,' he chuckled. 'How would you fancy having Bea as a step-mother?'

Kate flung her arms around him and

hugged him, hot tears welling in her eyes and spilling onto her cheeks. If her father found happiness here at Wyatt's Cove, then everything had been worthwhile. She said she was delighted, and clung to him until she had some control.

'Barbara Leon said she saw you at the show,' Kate said, wiping her eyes. 'She said you were having a great time.'

'I remember,' he said. 'Beautiful girl. Striking-looking.'

'That's the one,' Kate agreed.

'They're an unlikely pair,' David mused. 'There's Barbara, like a delicate china doll; then there's that man of hers, big and burly, with a thick black bushy beard and blazing blue eyes.'

Kate blinked. 'What are you talking about, Pa?'

'Ben Chatterton, the town's vet, and the brains behind the Summer Gala. He came here to look at Penny and asked me if I'd consider taking on the role of treasurer if he put my name forward.'

Kate shook her head. They must be

talking about different people, yet how many beautiful women by the name of Barbara lived in Wyatt's Cove? Obviously her father had somehow got hold of the wrong end of the stick.

'I don't think Ben Chatterton is Barbara's boyfriend, Pa,' she said.

'No, well he's obviously a bit more than that,' David agreed. 'I mean they live together in one of those tall terraces, the pink one I think. And I do believe a wedding is on the cards, because Ben said it was going to be difficult for him being a vet, being married to a woman who didn't much like dogs.'

Kate's mind was reeling. How could she have been so wrong all this time? And what had Barbara meant when she said that Cory would wear a top hat and tails for the wedding?

Suddenly it all slotted neatly into place. Cory must have some other role, best man perhaps, or maybe he was giving her away.

'Are you all right, Kate? You've gone all pale.'

'I'm just fine, Pa,' she said, stooping to drop a kiss on his cheek. 'Sleep well, darling, and I'll see you in the morning.'

Cory stood alone in the back garden, hands thrust deep into his pockets, just staring out to sea. She longed to tell him how she really felt, but how could she now? He probably wouldn't want anything to do with her and she wouldn't blame him.

'Are you giving Barbara away at her wedding?' she asked, her voice sounding like a whiplash in the peace of the night.

Cory turned and stared at her. The atmosphere between them was electrifying, but there was no relaxing of the tension in his jaw. His expression was giving nothing away and his eyes were as dark and cold as pebbles on the beach. Kate's heart ached with longing, but she couldn't cope with rejection, so was afraid to say what was in her heart.

At last he answered her, his voice as cold as his eyes. 'Yes, I am. Was that all you wanted to know?'

She hung her head and he strode towards her. For one wonderful, blissful moment, she thought he was going to hold her, but he brushed right past, his arm touching hers and sending shocks through her body.

Kate had never felt so cold, so shut out, so achingly unhappy. She turned and watched his retreating back and knew she couldn't let it end like this. 'I thought you were in love with Barbara,' she said shakily. 'I thought it was you she was marrying.'

Her voice halted him in his tracks and for an age he just stood there, his back to her, his stance totally uncompromising.

She wished she hadn't said it. Better to have let things die a natural death than try to revive anything. It was too late for all that now, much too late. She'd lost him through her own stupidity and could blame no one but herself. She had to bite hard on her lip to stop herself blurting out anything else as she stared at his rigid shoulders.

Then suddenly he was turning to face her. 'I do love Barbara,' he said. 'You don't go through all we went through together without forming a deep, abiding attachment. But I am not, and never have been, *in* love with her.' His voice was trembling as if he, too, was holding back, not saying all the things that so badly needed to be said. 'Besides, she's madly in love with Ben. Why, Kate?' he asked, his voice suddenly raw and tender. 'Does it make any difference?' All those messages she'd seen before in his eyes were back, and more intense than ever.

'Cory . . . ' She swallowed hard. Her mouth felt so dry. If it all went wrong now, if she said or did the wrong thing, she could lose him completely. 'That miracle you worked on my father — do you think it would work on me, too?'

'Oh, my love.' He came to her then, making short the distance between them as he pulled her into his arms, raining kisses down on her. 'I can try!'

His lips found hers and this time there was no resistance, no holding back as she melted against him, her body moulded to his as he crushed her in his embrace.

'Kate . . . ' He pushed her away a little and saw in her eyes the shining light of love. She looked almost drunk as she gazed up at him.

'I love you, Cory,' she whispered.

'I love you too, Kate,' he said and she closed her eyes, her heart singing, *I know, I know, I know.* And there were no more words between them.

★ ★ ★

A crisp breeze rustled the golden leaves on the trees and brought a cascade sweeping down across the church steps. Bea put up a hand to hold on to her broad-brimmed hat as she pushed David up the ramp and into the cool vestibule, where Kate and her bridesmaids waited. The dress had a full sweeping skirt and Kate had wondered how she would stop it being run over by her father's wheels. It didn't matter. What mattered was that he was here, looking dashing and distinguished in his grey morning coat.

'Everything all right, Kate?' he asked. 'He is here, isn't he?'

'I should hope so.' Kate laughed and peeped through a crack in the door. Cory was waiting at the front of the church, Ben Chatterton at his side. In a few minutes from now, they would take their vows and she would be his wife, a scenario she had never dared to even dream about a few short weeks ago.

Inside the church there was a lot of shuffling of hymn sheets, clearing of throats and a general air of anticipation. Unlike Barbara and Ben's quiet wedding in the summer, this was no quiet affair and the church was packed with well-wishers, some of whom Kate didn't even know.

'Ready?' Bea whispered and slipped into the church, hurrying to take her seat at the front. The vicar gave a signal and the peaceful organ music stopped and the bridal march was struck.

Kate drew back from the door and turned to face her father. 'Ready, Pa?' And she almost fell over. He was standing at her side, leaning heavily on a stick, but standing. He'd been having intensive sessions with Denise at the pool and the gym, but she had no idea his progress had been so tremendous.

'What's going on?' she cried, blinking, sure she must be dreaming.

'I always said I'd walk my little girl down the aisle one day,' he replied. 'And that's just what I intend to do.'

'But, Pa,' she protested, tears springing to her eyes. 'Are you sure? You don't have to do this.'

'Yes, I do. I've been practising,' he told her, and held out his arm for her to take. 'You might have to help me along a bit, but I've no intention of falling over and disgracing you.' He chuckled and Kate kissed him.

'I do love you, Pa,' she said, 'so very, very much.'

She trembled with pride as they entered the church and all eyes turned to face them. But the only eyes she could see, the only ones that mattered, were a pair of deep grey eyes, positively shining with love and directed straight at her. She loved him so much, she thought her heart would burst. As she drew level with him, he took her hand in his and kissed it, his lips sending delicious little tingles along her arm and down the length of her spine.

This was the beginning, their beginning, and Kate's heart was singing along with Cory's with the pure joy of being in love and the knowledge that the future was theirs.

THE END

We do hope that you have enjoyed
reading this large print book.

Did you know that all of our titles
are available for purchase?

We publish a wide range of high
quality large print books including:
Romances, Mysteries, Classics
General Fiction
Non Fiction and Westerns

Special interest titles available in
large print are:
The Little Oxford Dictionary
Music Book, Song Book
Hymn Book, Service Book

Also available from us courtesy of
Oxford University Press:
Young Readers' Dictionary
(large print edition)
Young Readers' Thesaurus
(large print edition)

For further information or a free
brochure, please contact us at:
Ulverscroft Large Print Books Ltd.,
The Green, Bradgate Road, Anstey,
Leicester, LE7 7FU, England.
Tel: (00 44) 0116 236 4325
Fax: (00 44) 0116 234 0205

Other titles in the
Linford Romance Library:

BORROWING ALEX

Cindy Procter-King

Nikki wants to get married more than anything. But what's she to do when her fiancé Royce is dragging his heels over setting a date? Why, fake a fling with the best man, of course! Ambushing Alex may be a tad desperate, but pretending she's hot for him just might kick-start Royce's attention . . . Alex is definitely not on board with this plan. But he quickly realizes Nikki isn't a wild party girl at all. She's cute, sweet — and faithful. Against his common sense, he's falling for her . . .